PRAISE FOR *NO SHAME, NO FEAR*

"An unusual and well-told story of love against the odds."
The Observer

"Here is a novel that needs a trumpet to be blown for it…
The pleasures lie less in plot surprises than in the plain, exact
and elegant language that takes you to the heart of each
character's feelings." *Adèle Geras, The Guardian*

"Historical details are deftly handled, building a rich picture
of momentous events set against personal, domestic lives,
particularly those of women. A pleasingly unexpected take
on the boy-meets-girl romance, set in a fascinating context."
Booktrusted News

"The unembellished but quietly passionate tone of the story
perfectly realizes the Quaker ideals of simplicity and truth,
and the privations which they endure with courage and
dignity serve to engage reader sympathy in a powerful,
understated way. Historical context is accurately and carefully used, but it is the measured tone of the narrative and its
humble, quiet characters with their rock of religion which
leave a lasting impression." *Books for Keeps*

"A novel of huge integrity told in a fittingly simple voice…
Turnbull has written a powerful and moving book that never
becomes shrill; she creates a past that is wholly credible and
sets out a thoughtful blueprint for tolerance."
Julia Eccleshare, The Guardian

"I was surprised to find how easily I was drawn inside this
gentle love story… This is a book for all teenagers and
adults who want to remind themselves how powerful
teenage passion can be." *Carousel*

FORGED IN THE FIRE

ANN TURNBULL

WALKER BOOKS
AND SUBSIDIARIES
LONDON · BOSTON · SYDNEY · AUCKLAND

This is a work of fiction. Names, characters, places
and incidents are either the product of the author's
imagination or, if real, are used fictitiously.

First published 2006 by Walker Books Ltd
87 Vauxhall Walk, London SE11 5HJ

2 4 6 8 10 9 7 5 3 1

Text © 2006 Ann Turnbull

Cover image based on *Portrait of a Woman* (oil on canvas), Henner,
Jean-Jacques (1829–1905) / Musée des Beaux-Arts, Mulhouse,
France, Giraudon / Bridgeman Art Library and
The Great Fire of London, 1666, Dutch School, (17th century) /
© Museum of London, UK / Bridgeman Art Library

Inside cover: *The Great Fire of London 1666* (woodcut) (b/w photo),
English School, (17th century) / © Museum of London, UK /
Bridgeman Art Library

The right of Ann Turnbull to be identified as author of this work
has been asserted by her in accordance with the
Copyright, Designs and Patents Act 1988

This book has been typeset in Cochin, Aqualine, Medici and
AT Marigold

Printed and bound in Great Britain by J.H. Haynes & Co. Ltd

British Library Cataloguing in Publication Data:
a catalogue record for this book
is available from the British Library

ISBN-13: 978-1-84428-935-6
ISBN-10: 1-84428-935-4

www.walkerbooks.co.uk

To Mara Bergman

William

For the hand of Susanna Thorn,
at Mary Faulkner's printing shop in Broad Street,
Hemsbury, in the County of Shropshire.
The third day of June, 1665.

Sweetheart: I write in haste, and in expectation of
being with thee soon after midsummer. I have
money enough saved now, and James Martell will
shortly give me leave of several weeks so that I may
return to Hemsbury and – if thou'rt willing –
bring thee back as my wife. Write to me soon, love,
and tell me that thou agree. Thou know how much
I miss thee. I think of thee every day and long to
hold thee in my arms again. Thy parents, thou
hast said, are willing for us to marry, and if thou

will speak to them and to the elders, we can be married in Eaton Bellamy Meeting as soon as may be arranged. As for my father, I fear there can be no reconciliation. He has never replied to my letters and I am not of a mind to ask his blessing now.

Make all straight with thy parents and the meeting, love, and with Mary; though I know she will not try to hold thee back. For my part, I cannot leave for a few weeks because my employer is still in poor health. We are both only recently out of prison; the business is in disorder and there is much to be done.

I shall use what free time I have to look for rooms for us, but will put money on nothing until thou hast seen it and agreed. Londoners live crowded together; there are many places to rent but not all are fitting. Nat and I lost our room in Pell Court when we were last in prison, so our address has changed again. We are now at Thomas Corder's, next to the Blue Boar in Creed Lane. The room is not so comfortable as the other, being cramped and ill-lit, but we have few needs and are both saving our wages: I to come to thee and be married, and Nat to set up in business on his own.

Nat will travel with me to Shropshire. He is homesick, I believe, and also wishes to see us married and to see Mary again. We plan to leave on the twenty-sixth of the month, and will travel on horseback with London Friends who are bound for Wales.

The weather here grows hotter by the day. They say there is plague in Holborn and St Giles, but we have none within the city walls. Pray God we shall be spared. Our Friends Robert Osman and Solomon Eccles go about the streets naked, crying repentance, as Dan Kite once did in Hemsbury. There is much talk of the city's evil and of God's wrath; but truly I believe there are many good people here.

I look forward to being outside the city soon, in the clean air of the countryside, coming closer to thee every day. Till then, love, may God keep thee safe.

Thy own,
Will Heywood

Susanna

"Mary!"

I burst into the print room with the letter in my hand – then stopped, and felt a blush rising as the men's faces turned towards me. My own face must have been alight with my news, for Mary guessed at once.

"He is coming, then?"

I nodded, speechless, so happy I feared I would cry.

"Well now, lass." John Pardoe gave me a fatherly hug. "Will's a lucky man to have such a loyal sweetheart. And thou'll be wed?"

"Yes. In a few weeks." I brushed at a tear, then turned to Mary. "We'll marry, he says, then go to London."

Mary regarded me gravely. My employer is not given to shows of emotion, but I saw that she was glad for me. "I shall miss thee," she said. "But thou hast earned thy happiness – and served out the time of thy agreement."

"Will says Nat will come too."

Everyone – but Mary especially – was pleased at this news. Nat had been Mary's apprentice; she'd come to look on him almost as a son. There was a brief outbreak of talk and reminiscence, but soon Mary called the men back to work, and I left them.

Mary's printworks includes a bookshop and stationer's, and that was where I'd been when the post boy came – unpacking a box of new books from Oxford and listing their titles. I returned to this task; but after a while, there being no customers in the shop, I took out the letter and read it again, several times.

Until now I had been content with my lot, saving my wages and waiting to hear this news from Will. But now, when I knew that soon I would see him again, it was as if a river had burst its banks: my feelings overflowed, and I felt a great surge of longing and impatience. I wanted to leave and fly to him at once – to meet him on the road; to be married immediately; to hold and kiss him again.

I brought his remembered face to mind – and not only his face, but the feel of him: his arms around me, his warmth, his voice, his kisses. I had no portrait of him, nothing but those memories. He would have changed, I knew. He was a scholar when I met him, but for the last three years he'd been working for a bookseller in London. Like me, he'd been in prison for his beliefs – for meeting to worship with Friends – and had become stronger in spirit as a result; I knew that much from his letters. We must both have changed. He'd be twenty now, and I was eighteen. We were still young for marriage, but we had proved we could wait for each other.

Did I appear different too, I wondered? What would he think of me? We'd communicated for so long by letter, and had come to know each other's minds, but in all that time we had met only once, in the autumn of 1663, in Oxford, where there had been a gathering of the Friends of Truth. Will had gone there with his employer, and I had contrived to go too, travelling with Friends from Hemsbury. Will and I had been determined to seize the opportunity to meet, if only for a moment, and in truth it was little more than that, for we were among large groups of people and staying at different inns. We spent no more than an hour together, walking by the river, but it was enough to reaffirm our love for each other, to bind us. That day in Oxford we vowed we would be married in two years' time, when my term of service with Mary ended.

I thought of the marriage of my friends Judith Minton and Daniel Kite, which had taken place soon after Will left for London. They had made their promises to each other at a meeting in the parlour of William Jevons's house, with Friends crowded in, some on benches, younger ones on the floor – all risking arrest, for any gathering of Quakers, as folk call us, is unlawful. My own marriage had seemed a far-away hope then, but now I imagined being with Will legitimately, with no one to hinder us; living with him as his wife, in our own home.

Mary came into the shop, startling me, and I turned guiltily to the box of books.

She smiled. "Thou must go home for first-day, Susanna. Stay a day or two with thy parents, and ask their blessing."

"I will."

But today I wanted to see Judith.

I soon found an excuse to go out.

One of the books that had arrived that morning was for our Friend John Callicott, who lives in Cord-wainer Row, off the High Street. I could have sent the boy, Antony, with it, but instead I told Mary I'd deliver it myself.

The way there took me past the Heywood family home, on the corner of High Street and Butcher's Row. As always when I passed it, I glanced in through the entrance to the courtyard, where some-times carts were drawn up and bales of wool loaded or delivered. Last week I'd seen Henry Heywood, Will's father. My breath had quickened, and I'd hurried past. But his back was towards me; he didn't see me, and probably would not have known me if he had. I was nothing to him: merely that "little whore" who'd set out to entrap his son. He could not know of our plans to marry, since he had cut Will off and would accept no letters from him.

Today the courtyard was empty. I passed the long warehouse on the ground floor and hurried on up the High Street.

My delivery done, I went to find Judith. As I'd guessed, she was not at her own home, but with her mother, in the family's glove shop in the High Street. Abigail, her sister, was serving in the shop. She sent me through to the workroom at the back, where Judith and her mother, Elinor, sat stitching gloves and talking – Judith rocking, with one foot, the Minton family cradle in which she had placed her son.

"Susanna!"

They stood up, surprised and pleased to see me in work time. Elinor called to their servant, Hester, to fetch small beer.

"No, I can't stay," I said. But I bent down to admire the baby. This was Judith's second child. Her first, a girl, had died soon after birth, causing her great grief. Young Benjamin looked well. He was two months old, and tightly swaddled, but his eyes – bright blue like his father's – followed my movements; and I thought I saw a trace of a smile.

"Oh, he does smile!" Judith assured me.

I smiled too. "I am happy for thee," I said. "And for myself." I told them my news.

Judith put down her work and embraced me, and Elinor said, "God bless thee, Susanna!" and hurried out to tell Hester and Abigail, leaving us to talk.

"I'm afraid Will might see me differently after those London girls," I admitted to Judith. "A country lass. I fear things may have changed between us. I don't know him now."

"But you write to each other. Thou know his heart."

"Yes." We wrote constantly, often by return. I had come to live for the post. But it was not enough. I needed to touch him, to hold him, to be sure. And I wondered if he had similar fears; if he regretted our promises.

"It will all be as before when you see each other," Judith reassured me. And she added, "Dan and I will still be here for your wedding."

I knew that Dan and Judith planned to sail to America, to Massachusetts, later in the summer.

"We have booked our passage," said Judith. "We leave for Bristol in August, and sail on the eighteenth."

There was an expression akin to defiance on her face.

I looked at the child, then at her.

"He is so tiny – so precious to thee," I said. I wanted to ask how she could think of sailing to America, to undertake such a dangerous journey to an unknown new life, now that she had a child. But that was between her and Daniel.

"It will be easier now than later," said Judith. "The babe is not weaned, so I shall not have to fear the shipboard food; and he cannot yet crawl and get into danger."

"And dost thou want to go?"

"My husband wants to go. And I knew he did when I agreed to marry him. I don't doubt I could persuade him to stay here, but I won't. It would diminish him."

"Thy mother will miss thee – and the babe."

"Ha! My mother says I have made my bed and must lie in it. She warned me that I would never have an easy life with Daniel. And yet she understands him, I think, and believes that God has called him to this. It's his own mother who is distraught at losing her grandchild. She berates Dan every time she sees him." Her voice quivered, and she bit her thumbnail. "We shall be so far apart, Su; thou in London and I in America."

"But we'll write." I had taught both Judith and Abigail to write a little, passing on the skills I'd learned from Mary.

"Yes," agreed Judith. "We will. And tell all. All our hopes and prayers. And our babies."

Babies. It gave me a jolt to think that I too would soon have babies if I married Will. I had often day-dreamed of having children in the future, but now it drew near: real, enticing, and yet to be feared.

I went home to Long Aston on seventh-day. The roads were rough underfoot, but dry and passable after the long spell of fine weather we'd had. A farmer offered me a ride on his cart, and I was glad of it, for the weather was too warm for walking. In the fields the lambs were almost full-grown, and the hedgerows dense and green and full of pale pink dog roses. I wanted to remember it all, for I guessed I'd see no such sights in London.

The farmer set me down a mile and a half from home, and I walked there through the meadows, and picked daisies and made a chain; then crossed the stream by the stepping stones that led into the wood, and so up to our yard the back way.

Deb was there, spreading washing to dry on the bushes. She was growing up fast, and looked taller, I thought, every time I came home. When she saw me she shouted in delight and ran to meet me.

"I thought thou weren't coming till next week!"

"Mary let me come. I have news."

"Oh, Su! What? What news? Is it about Will? Is he coming? Tell me!"

"Wait!" I said, laughing, and tossed the daisy chain over her head. I had never felt happier. I shall bring him here, I thought. He had never visited my parents' home, though they had met him, once, at Mary's shop, before he left for London. I'd show him the stream, and the path up to Overton, and the Disbury Maze where they say the fairies dance at new moon, and that grassy place at the edge of the wood where I'd once guiltily imagined lying with him, long ago…

I heard the clacking of my father's loom, and then my mother appeared and gave a cry of joy – "Husband! Susanna is here!" – and the loom stopped.

My father came out, and I was caught up in their embraces and questions.

My mother exclaimed, "Thou'rt early! I told Isaac he should come home next week and thou'd be here."

And my father, with his grave smile, chided her. "Be thankful to see the girl now."

"Su has news!" said Deb. Her face was eager. She has wide-set blue eyes, like our mother, and the same square chin, while Isaac and I are brown-eyed and take after our father.

I gave them my news. My parents were glad for me – though not surprised, since they had known we planned to marry as soon as I was free and Will settled in work, and with prospects. I had told them before that James Martell liked him well and intended in a year or two to bring him into the business.

"Then that would be the time to marry," my father had said. "You are both still too young as yet."

But my mother had prevailed. "They have waited three years," she said, "and stayed true. Think how lightly we lived, husband, when we were young! Let them have their time together."

Now, my father said only that we must both think of the responsibilities of marriage, and seek God's help in the silence. "And tomorrow, Susanna, as Will is not here, thou must speak to the meeting alone and tell them of thy wish to be married."

"I will."

I feared to have the meeting's attention all on me, but there was no likelihood that they would not approve, since my parents were willing.

My mother sent Deb to fetch a jug of small beer from the inn. There was a pottage simmering over the fire, and she ladled us out a bowlful each, and served it with bread and herbs.

Later, she took me aside, opened the big oak chest in which we had always kept our clothes and bedding, and brought out something wrapped in worn sheeting. She shook it out.

It was a woman's shift, with a high neckline and long sleeves, such as I would wear under my skirt and bodice, or in bed. The linen was fine and soft, bleached to a pale oat colour, and it was neatly and plainly stitched; without lace, for Friends do not wear such decoration, but with a narrow border of feather stitch, in the same oat colour, marking the hems.

I had never owned such a fine shift. I turned to my mother in gratitude. "Thou made it?"

"And thy father wove the linen and bleached it. It is a gift for thy marriage."

I stroked the cloth, thinking of the hours of work, often by rushlight. "I thank thee, Mam."

My mother held her work against me, to check the length; and I thought: I'll be wearing this shift on my wedding night. My face grew warm, and I was aware of Deb watching me.

Next day we walked to Meeting. Eaton Bellamy Meeting is held in Lewis Streetley's great barn, and we settled on benches and straw bales in the lofty space with its smells of hay and leather, and chickens scratching around the doorway. This barn was the place where I loved best to meet and had always felt closest to God. As the silence fell, I imagined standing here with Will, making our promises each to be a loving and faithful partner to the other until death should separate us. Then I tried to draw my thoughts inward as I felt the meeting become gathered.

Out of the silence, several Friends spoke of the love and power of God. Towards the end, as people began to shift in their seats, I took courage and spoke in a low, nervous voice of my desire and Will's to be married. They listened without speaking, but afterwards many came and said they would be glad to witness our marriage, and I knew I had the love of the meeting.

As we walked home, my mother said, "You may stay at the inn at Long Aston, thou and Will, since you'll have no home of your own to go to. Thy father will pay. And the Streetleys will host the wedding breakfast."

She tried to speak cheerfully, but she looked pensive, and I knew she was thinking that soon after the wedding, Will and I would go to London – and none of us knew how long it would be before we might meet again.

But I could not share her gloom. Will's letter had taken nearly a week to reach me. In only two weeks' time he would leave London; and with hired horses they would travel fast. Soon we would be together.

"We will come back, Mam," I said. "I promise thee. And I'll write often, and tell thee all that happens in the city."

She touched my face gently. "Pray God Will takes good care of thee there."

The next day I returned to Hemsbury, to my work. As I folded and cut pamphlets, hung up printed sheets and dealt with customers, I thought much about my coming role as a wife.

I told all my friends – Martha and Kezia Jevons, Grace Heron, Em Taylor – and wrote to my brother, Isaac, who was apprenticed to a weaver in Bristol. The days crept by. Once midsummer was past, I would look up, heart thumping, every time there was a knock at the door; and I got into the habit, each evening, of walking down to the East Bridge and gazing out along the road in hope of seeing them coming.

The long days dragged.

"They will come in God's good time," said Mary.

But I was in a fever of anxiety and expectation. I feared illness, or some accident on the road. Newssheets from London told of war with Holland; the navy hard-pressed; plague increasing and spreading into the heart of the city.

At last, two weeks after they should have arrived,

I heard Mary calling me. I was upstairs, and the urgency in her voice made me race down into the kitchen, alight with hope.

"Are they here?"

But Mary was alone. There was an acid smell in the room that caught at the back of my throat, and I saw that she was holding a letter over a small pan of boiling liquid.

I turned weak with fear. A letter now could only mean bad news.

"For me?" I asked. "From Will?"

"Yes."

"What are you doing?" I reached out for it.

"We are warned to air letters from London over boiling vinegar, to avoid contagion."

Terror leaped in my heart. The plague. Please God, I thought, not Will.

"The ink will run!" I almost snatched the letter from her. "Let me see! Oh, Mary, what does he say?"

William

Less than two weeks before Nat and I were due to leave London, I walked down towards Blackfriars to look at some rooms for rent. It was evening, warm, and still sunny, and I had left work and arranged to meet Nat later and go to an alehouse for dinner. We had little means to cook at our lodgings; it was easier to buy pies, bread and fruit in the street markets, or occasionally to pay our landlady for a bowl of pottage.

I had looked at several places in recent days, but liked none of them. They might do for me, I felt, but not for Susanna. Nat and I had got into bachelor ways. I could not imagine Susanna, so clean and orderly as I remembered her, trapped in such poor rooms without means to cook or wash linen. This latest was cleaner and more spacious, but I feared the rent was too high; I said I would think on it.

I left, and began walking to Ludgate Hill, where I had arranged to meet Nat at the Crown. On the way, I daydreamed about having Susanna here with me. Often, as I walked around the city, I imagined showing her the sights: the river, the great ships being unloaded at the wharves, Cheapside, the shops on London Bridge, and all the new books that came to James Martell's shop. But today I imagined the two of us in just such a room as I'd seen, naked in bed together, warm with love.

I was lost in these pleasurable thoughts when I reached the corner of Shoemaker Row – and pulled up in shock.

A soldier was lounging in the doorway of a house, his halberd propped beside him. It was a good-sized house, well kept, such as a successful tradesman might inhabit. But the door was chained and barred. On it was painted a red cross, with a printed notice nailed beside it: *Lord have mercy upon us*.

The sight sent a chill through me. Every summer that I remembered, whether in Shropshire, Oxford, or London, there had been deaths from plague; but I had never given it much thought, knowing it to afflict mainly the poor, who live crowded together in verminous conditions. And although I had heard of houses being enclosed and having the cross painted on their doors, it was a thing I had never seen before. Now I was struck, not with fear – for I felt too strong and alive to contract the sickness – but with horror and compassion to think that anyone should come to such a plight. The dead would have been removed, and those surviving would now be locked up for a month in the foul air of the house of sickness until the risk of contagion was over.

Nat was already at the Crown when I arrived. I observed him for a moment before he saw me, and understood why we Friends were usually recognized as such by other people, often before we spoke. There was something about his plain coat and rather old-fashioned hat, together with a quiet look of inward retirement, that marked him out. And yet Nat was not a solemn man. He had a quick smile that brightened his face when he turned and saw me.

"The rooms?" he asked.

"Fair. But too high a rent."

"Thou can look about when she is here."

"Yes."

I sat down on the bench opposite him. Our Friends the Palmers had said Susanna could stay with them as long as she liked. But until we found rooms we could not live together as man and wife. Nat knew that.

"Thou'll find somewhere quick enough when the time comes," he said, with a wink.

We laughed. Men near by glanced our way, but no one troubled us. We had found people mostly to be more tolerant in London than in the country, and we were rarely threatened except by the authorities, who were zealous at breaking up meetings.

We ordered beer, and fish cooked in a pastry coffin. The girl who served us allowed her glance to flick between the two of us. She had dark, teasing eyes, and we were both conscious of her appraisal.

When she had gone I said, "I saw a house enclosed – the cross on the door."

"I heard folk here speaking of it. So the plague is on our doorstep now."

We'd both read the Bills of Mortality that were posted around the city every week, but that freshly painted cross, in its blood-red starkness, acted more forcibly on my imagination than any words. We were due to leave the city soon; I'd be glad to get away. Perhaps by the time we returned the danger would have passed.

The girl came back with our food, and I asked if she knew who lived in the enclosed house.

She was only too willing to tell. "Thomas Richmond, a shipping clerk," she said. "Sickened and died within five days. And now his wife and four little children shut up, poor souls." She put a hand to her bosom, where I had noticed a sprig of something was tucked. "I keep a bunch of wormwood and rue always about me; and take plague waters…" She glanced at Nat. "You work for Amos Bligh, the Quaker printer, don't you?"

He nodded. "I do."

"I've seen you about. Take care with the pastry – it's hot."

She left, and we caught each other's eye and smiled.

The pastry was indeed hot, and we burned our fingers breaking it open. The fish inside was spiced with cardamom and nutmeg. We ate with relish, and felt glad to be alive. The plague was in the city – but danger was always present. We must go about our lives as usual, and trust in God.

During the next week, however, I began to feel a greater sense of urgency to be away. On the Bill of Mortality the figure for plague deaths had risen. I saw another house with the cross on the door, this time near Cheapside, in the heart of the city. Plague orders were posted all around: every householder was to keep the street before his door swept clean; large gatherings of people were banned (they'd use this to break up Friends' meetings, I knew); the playhouses were closed; the great fairs – Bartholomew and James's – would not be held. I had no interest in fairs and playhouses, and yet these restrictions on our liberty made me more afraid than anything else.

"You and Nat Lacon should leave the city as soon as possible," my employer said.

We were in his bookshop in Paul's Churchyard, in the shadow of the great steeple-house. I had been out delivering an order to a customer in Fleet Street, and had seen an apothecary come out of a house wearing a waxed cloak and a long pointed mask, like a bird's beak.

"It is to protect him when he visits those sick with the plague," James had explained. "The beak is filled with purifying herbs."

He was old enough to remember such sights – terrifying to a child – from the last great outbreak of plague in London, forty years ago.

Dorcas, the Martells' young maidservant, had set vases of rue and rosemary around the shop to freshen the air, and there were bowls of vinegar on the counter for customers to drop the coins into. But otherwise all seemed reassuringly normal. Cecily, James's wife, was serving in the stationery section, and from the back of the shop I could hear a child's voice: their eldest, six-year-old Agnes, reading a story to her brother.

I said, "Thou hast more need than I to leave – with thy wife and children."

"We have nowhere else to go. All Cecily's people live in the city, and I have only a brother in Aldgate. We shall stay here, and trust in God's mercy. Cecily is of the same mind."

Cecily was James's second wife, much younger than he, and the mother of his young family. They were serious, sober people with a great love of books and learning. They had taken me on when I first arrived in London and given me work in their business – which thrived because James was known for his knowledge and honest dealing.

"I promised I would stay till the twenty-sixth," I said.

"Thou need not concern thyself. It is a matter of days only, and I am well enough now. But the authorities may begin to restrict travel. Already they say towns outside the city grow nervous of receiving Londoners. Leave while thou can. Go to thy sweetheart."

He smiled. And indeed he looked much recovered, and I knew his health need not hold me back.

I walked through the shop, passing the children, who were curled up together with a chapbook of Robin Hood. They sat on the floor in one of the bays between tall shelves of books, and Agnes paused shyly in her reading as I went by, then continued. *"'By my faith,' quoth bold Robin, 'here cometh a merry fellow…'"*

I went to the desk where I kept records, and entered my delivery and the payment in a ledger. Agnes and Stephen watched me, glancing up from the book. They were quiet children, never troublesome; soft-spoken like their parents and able to amuse themselves. The family and Dorcas lived above the shop, but James and Cecily liked to allow the children downstairs, where, they said, they would gain a sense of right livelihood from the earliest age.

The children, I guessed, simply enjoyed all the places to hide and whisper. The shop was large and rambling, with many hundreds of books, pamphlets, and writings of Friends, and deliveries and orders coming all the time from Belgium and France, as well as English towns and cities. Nearly half the space was given over to stationery: quills, ink, notebooks and printed forms – a much greater selection than I had ever seen in Mary Faulkner's shop in Hemsbury. James kept books of almost every kind – not plays, since he disapproved of the theatre, but poetry and music as well as theological and historical writings.

Back at work, I put the sight of the beaked man out of my mind, but next morning I talked to Nat.

"It seems cowardly to leave early."

From near by we heard the bells of Gregory's steeple-house tolling, and counted six for a woman, and then the years of her life: twenty – my own age. Was it plague, I wondered? And now that I thought of it, I heard other passing bells, many more than usual, further away, from all around the city.

Nat was at the washbowl, a mirror propped up, shaving. He had cut his long curly hair and paid Meg Corder to wash and iron some shirts for the journey. I had bought a new shirt to be married in. We had little else to do before we left. I felt a strong desire to leave at once. And yet we were committed to travelling with our friends.

"I spoke to Joseph Leighton," Nat said, rubbing his face dry, and wincing at a cut. "He says we need not wait for them."

"Can they not leave earlier than the twenty-sixth?"

"No. Their affairs prevent it."

The Leighton brothers were elderly men, frail from prolonged imprisonment, yet alight with the spirit. They had felt called to visit Friends in prison in North Wales. For us to travel with them would be beneficial to all. We would have their company and the hire of horses, and would probably eat better and sleep more comfortably than if we travelled alone; and they would have our youth and strength should need arise.

Nat voiced my thoughts. "It would be churlish not to wait for them."

I agreed. "Yes. For the sake of a week…"

And yet I wanted nothing more than to leave the stricken city. And we were ready; our employers would give us leave; we had nothing to hold us back, except our promise. To my shame, I felt irritation with the old men; what affairs could they possibly have that would take so long to set in order?

During the days that followed, the sense of crisis in the city grew apace. Everyone was leaving who could. We saw carts loaded with families and their possessions rumbling through the streets towards the city gates. A house was enclosed in Creed Lane, where we lived, making Nat and I feel, for the first time, afraid for our lives. Meanwhile the Leighton brothers calmly hired horses, received messages and parcels from Friends to be delivered along the way, and arranged with us to leave early in the morning on the twenty-sixth of the month.

But a few days before we were due to leave, we saw a new notice being posted at the conduit. It said that from now on travel out of the city would be permitted only if the traveller was in possession of a Certificate of Health; this to be obtained from the minister and churchwardens of his parish, and signed and sealed by a Justice of the Peace.

The news must have flown around the city. Nat and I went at once with the Leightons to see what could be done, and joined a long queue of desperate people. We soon discovered that few certificates were being granted and that it helped if you were known to the minister. All dissidents – Presbyterians, Baptists and the like – were given short shrift; but Friends in particular, who refused to pay church tithes, had no chance. We came away, after many hours, empty-handed.

"We will try again," said Joseph Leighton, "another day."

So we waited; and tried again, but without success. Money might have moved matters along, but we would not offer bribes. We were accused, as Quakers, of consorting with felons, and gathering in large and unlawful numbers in close rooms where the pestilence might breed. And perhaps the churchwardens were right, for on first-day we learned that a family from our meeting, the Ansons, had the sickness, and had voluntarily enclosed themselves. All of us must have been aware, though we did not speak of it, that only last week we had been in the same room as Matthias Anson, breathing the same air. Two of the older women, Jane Catlin and Ann Hale, said they would go in and take care of the Ansons until the end, whether that was recovery or death. Then we were silent and prayed for them.

Few of our meeting were able to leave; and of those who could, many would not, feeling it to be desertion – that they should stay and help those who suffered, and trust in God. I had no such scruples. All I wanted now was to reach Shropshire, to reach Susanna. I could not help regretting how far I was now from my father's power and protection. A man of his standing would have had me out of the city without delay.

The twenty-sixth of June – the day we should have left – came and went. Another Friend, related to a magistrate, made an attempt on our behalf to gain certificates, but perhaps the news of the Ansons' sickness made us suspect; again we were refused. The Leighton brothers accepted the change to their plans, and abandoned them for the time being. Their desire to leave London was less urgent than ours. Nat, too, was philosophical, though disappointed. But I railed against fate, and felt desperate. It was like being in prison again. I imagined storybook escapes: a counterfeit certificate; or hiding under the goods in a carrier's cart.

On fourth-day in the first week of July, all Londoners were commanded to attend church and pray for God's mercy and a release from the pestilence; markets, shops and taverns were to close. James Martell closed the shop, and we joined Friends as usual at Meeting. The authorities did not molest us. It was a quiet day that gave me hope.

Indeed, all this time, I hoped against reason that the plague would abate, the emergency come to an end, and then Nat and I could be on our way to Shropshire. But then the King and court left the city for the safety of Isleworth; and about the same time, an order went out that all cats and dogs were to be killed, for fear they should carry the contagion from house to house. It was when I saw men going about the streets clubbing to death every cat or dog in sight that I realized we were on the brink of a calamity which had only just begun.

And so, at last, I took Nat's advice to write a letter to Susanna and attempt to send it by post before that too should fail.

Susanna

Love, don't fear if thou hear nothing from me for a
while. The authorities may restrict the post – and
even if they do not, I may hesitate to write to thee
for fear the carrier should be infected. Take care to
steam any letters from London over boiling
vinegar; we are assured it is a preventive...

"How can I not fear?" I demanded of Judith. I had
run to her in my distress. "The plague is in the city,
in their street, in their meeting. Oh, Judith, I am so
afraid he will die and I will never see him again!"

Judith put her arms around me and begged me not
to despair. As she tried to comfort me, I was reminded
of how helpless I had felt in the face of her own over-
whelming grief when her first child died. But Will was

not dead. I had lost nothing yet, except the chance to be married this summer – as Judith reminded me.

"The plague will go when the hot weather is over," she said, "and then he will come, and all will be well. Truly, Su, it will."

We were in the parlour of Judith's small house in Castle Street. It reminded me of my parents' house, with the curtained bed and oak storage chest in the parlour, and a hall and kitchen off. Judith had been shelling peas, and the sweet smell of opened pea pods scented the room. Benjamin was asleep in his cradle.

I wiped my eyes, ashamed of my weakness. "I did so long to be married."

Mary had shown less patience with me than Judith. She'd told me sharply to be busy about my work and to thank God I had heard no bad news as yet. What concerned her more was news from London of Friends dying in Newgate jail, and of some who awaited transportation to the West Indies. There was much talk in our meetings now of the changes which had come in last year to the Quaker Act, which made meeting for worship punishable by transportation for a third offence, and which did away with the necessity for a jury. Our Friends were writing pamphlets; and reports of the injustices meted out to Friends around the country were printed in Mary's shop. Some of these reports came from the meeting that Will and Nat attended, at the Bull and Mouth tavern in Aldersgate. I knew this meeting to be large and active and a thorn in the flesh of the authorities, who made regular swoops upon it, throwing many Friends into jail. Will and Nat, and their employers, had all been imprisoned for several months at the end of last year. I'd had no letters then from Will himself, and heard news of him only from his employer's wife, Cecily Martell.

I kept all my letters in the chest in my room above the shop – for I still lived with Mary Faulkner, though I no longer shared her bedchamber as a servant. My room was next to Mary's, and had formerly been Nat's when he was her apprentice. It was small, and simply furnished, with a bed, chest, chair and wash-stand; but I felt proud to be a working woman with a room of my own. I hung my two spare gowns on pegs on the wall and kept everything else – my linen, stock-ings, books, letters and money – in the chest. The clothes were stored with herbs between the layers, so that whenever I took out Will's letters – as I did often – they smelled of rosemary and lavender.

Next time I went home to my parents I was enfolded in their sympathy and that of Eaton Bellamy Meeting. Friends told me to have faith, not to des-pair, but to accept God's will; and I tried to do that. As the weeks went by I worked hard, printing and delivering, inking the type, checking proofs, serving in the shop – even setting up the type if Simon Race was busy. I also instructed the boy, Antony – nine years old, and an orphan, one of the parish poor, as Nat had been when Mary took him on.

But no amount of work could make me forget; I longed for a letter, some proof that Will was alive. When he was in prison I had still had news of him, but now there was nothing. Nothing from Will, or Nat, or even Cecily Martell. I began to fear that they were all dead. The news was unreliable. There were fewer travellers now to bring it, and people were uneasy about receiving news-sheets from London. But rumour told of a city from which King and court had gone; where half the shops were shut; where kites and crows circled above graveyards heaped high with burials, and bodies were no longer carried on pallets but collected by the load in carts.

At the beginning of August, Judith and Daniel prepared to leave for Bristol to begin their journey to the New World. I was about to lose my closest friend, and my spirits sank still lower. The last meeting they attended was held in Samuel Minton's workroom, with the leather cuttings cleared away, the tables stacked, and extra benches brought in. The meeting, though large, was not disturbed by the sheriff's men – for which we were thankful. Of late our meetings had been less often disrupted. Robert Danson, that sheriff who had been so forward in persecuting us, had been struck down by God last year with an apoplexy and had died. His replacement was a man who saw that the townsfolk were for the most part willing to tolerate Dissenters, and therefore acted only when provoked. But in London, we heard, persecution continued.

Several Friends spoke of the horrors visited upon London, and attributed it to God's judgement on a court and people grown corrupt, greedy and licentious, and who persecuted the innocent. One (who did not have a loved one there) spoke so, and with such self-righteousness that I almost jumped to my feet and retorted, as Will had said to me in his letter, that London's soul was not lost: there were many good people there. But I missed my moment, and sat silent, my heart hammering with the unspoken words.

Then Dan stood up. As usual, he spoke in pictures.

"Friends, you know I am a blacksmith, and work with iron and fire. The iron softens in the fire, and changes its nature; it can be moulded to any shape the smith desires. But first it must be heated till it glows red-hot; it must go through the fire. I see us, Friends, like that iron. We have suffered; we have been in the red-hot heart of the fire. And through our suffering we have changed and grown strong in spirit. We have been forged in the fire, and will endure, come what may…"

He went on to speak of how he felt called to reach out to the New World. "In our meetings here I have been filled with the presence of the living God. And the Word of God has called on me to proclaim to others what I have experienced. I must go across land and sea to the far places of the earth and labour in the service of the gospel."

The next day they left: Dan, Judith and the baby. Dan had hired a cart, and they took an oak chest containing all their belongings, a basket of food for the journey, and letters and bundles for Friends in Bristol – in particular Judith's brother Tom and my brother, Isaac, who were both apprentices there.

As the cart was being loaded everyone wished them well and sent blessings with them. But Judith and I threw our arms around each other and cried. We knew this would probably be the last time we ever met.

"Oh, Su, I wish I could have left thee happier! I'll give thy letter to Isaac – I have it here. And write to me when thou hear from Will. Promise? Write straight away!"

"I will," I said, though we both knew any news sent to America would arrive months later.

Dan embraced me too, and I kissed the babe. Then

Dan sprang up and reached down his hand for Judith, and Elinor handed up Benjamin to them.

They looked a fine couple: Judith tall, fair and gentle, with her child in her arms; Dan broad and strong. They were going into the unknown, perhaps into danger and persecution; and yet I wished, at that moment, that I was Judith, setting off with my husband for a new life.

William

"That cat has pissed behind the door again," I said.

Nat had just come in from work, grimy with ink, his shirt showing sweat stains on the back and under the arms, his hair stuck to his forehead.

"It can't smell worse than I do."

He pulled the shirt off and flung it into a corner, then washed himself in the water I'd left in the bowl after coming in equally hot and sweaty.

The room was stifling. It was on the ground floor, with one small window that opened onto a shared backyard and passageway. I pushed it further open, but there was no fresh air, only the stench from the communal privy.

Nat and I had had words about the cat before. It was one of our landlord's, but Nat had taken charge of it when the order went out that all cats and dogs were to be killed. It was big with kittens, and he'd shut it in our room for safety. Meg Corder must have known it was there, for it miaowed relentlessly and scratched to be let out.

"It craps on the floor," I said. "It eats our food. And it always sleeps on *my* bed."

The cat was on my bed now, one leg in the air, cleaning its arse. I clapped my hands at it, and it sprang off and made its way to Nat's abandoned shirt, where it turned around a few times and then curled up, purring.

Nat pulled a mock-apologetic face. I tried to remain angry, but broke out in a laugh.

"I'll get a type tray from work," Nat said, "and put some earth in it. And empty it – I promise!"

"I'm sorry," I said. "It's the heat."

From midsummer onwards the heat had been intense. We were all trapped in the city as in a cauldron of fire, with scarce enough air to breathe. The gutters and cesspits stank, the Fleet River was foul with sewage, the marketplaces reeked of rotting fruit and vegetables; and underlying every other smell was the sickly-sweet odour of decaying corpses. The authorities were struggling to cope with the increasing numbers of dead, but even lime could not dispose of them fast enough, and the graveyards were piled high.

The Bills of Mortality showed seven hundred and fifty deaths from plague in one week. Our Friends the Ansons, who had voluntarily enclosed themselves, were the first in our meeting to suffer. Their maid, Ellin Crowe, died first; then Mary Anson; her husband; and their young apprentice, Roger Millard, newly come from Canterbury. Matthias Anson's house and shop, which had been a carpenter's, was shut up. It would be cleansed and fumigated when all danger of plague had passed. The two Friends who had cared for them, Jane Catlin and Ann Hale, were sisters, both widows who lived alone. Ann took sick a week later and died within five days; but Jane was spared, though she kept herself apart for the allotted time.

These deaths caused much sadness in our meeting and caused us all to think about our own mortality. I thanked God that I had not, after all, brought Susanna into this afflicted city. And yet, despite everything, I wanted her with me. I longed to be living with her in rooms of our own instead of here with Nat. I knew that part of my irritation with him came from that sense of having been thwarted in my desires.

Like most people, my employer found that his business was affected. The shop was not as busy as before, with most of his wealthy customers gone, but that gave us leisure to sort and catalogue the stock, and for James to attend to some of the business of our meeting. He wrote to several families about their loss: the parents of Roger Millard and Ellin Crowe, and the widowed father of Mary Anson; and corresponded with Friends in other London meetings. We heard news: that our Friend George Fox remained in prison in Lancaster; and that the authorities at Newgate prison were still seeking a captain willing to undertake the transportation of those Friends sentenced to banishment to Jamaica for seven years. It cheered us to know that most captains would have nothing to do with the transportation of Friends, their natural inclinations turning them against such unjust work.

The Martell children, Agnes and Stephen, were too young to understand these matters – though Agnes listened, with a troubled face, to her parents' talk, and often asked questions. Most days they ran about the shop, playing hide-and-seek between the stacks of books, and watching us go about our work.

"What's that big book?" Agnes asked me once, pointing out one bound in dark green leather with gold lettering and a design of flowers and trellis-work embossed in gold on the spine.

"That is Plutarch," I said. "A Roman. He wrote biographies of famous men."

Agnes traced the gold with her finger. "Will thou read it to us?"

"I fear you would find it very dull." But I could see that the beauty of the book fascinated her.

"I shall learn to read it," she said.

Stephen reached out too, but Agnes pushed his hand away. "No, Stephen. Thou'rt sticky."

Stephen wailed in protest. I put the book away and the tears subsided. He stuck his thumb in his mouth and lolled against me. "Tib's gone," he said. "Bad men took him."

"Tib?" I had seen carts laden with the corpses of cats and dogs rattling through the streets on their way to a dump outside the city wall.

"They are not bad men," I said. "They hope to keep us all safe from the plague. But we have a cat at home who will soon have kittens. When the contagion is over I will ask our landlord if you may have one, if your mother agrees."

"Will it have white paws?" asked Stephen.

"Silly!" said Agnes. "Only God knows that."

But I said to Stephen, "It might."

Agnes was uncertain whether she wanted another cat. "I loved Tib," she said.

The following week there was scarcely a cat or dog to be seen in the streets, and rats were everywhere.

The gentry had fled the city for their country homes. The Royal Exchange used to be a place where the wealthy came to be seen, and to buy trinkets, perfumes, gloves and lace. Now the great space was almost bare of people, half the shops closed. Only the markets and most of the everyday shops in Poultry, Pudding Lane and Cheapside continued as before.

And yet nothing was as before. People had changed towards each other. We had all begun to keep to the middle of the streets – even walking in the filth of the central gutter to keep clear of whatever airs or foul breath might waft from buildings. And I believe we all looked each other over, every time we met, for the first signs of plague: sweat, pallor and chill. The sight of houses with the red cross on the door had become commonplace – as had the sound of people within screaming in agony. Cecily, returning from market one day, burst into the shop, overcome with guilt. "I saw a man leap from an upper window in a plague house!" she said. "Stark naked and raving with pain. He charged like a mad animal and beat his head against the wall and fell dying. Everyone scattered. God forgive me, but I left him; I ran; I was so afraid…"

It was on fifth-day of that week, when I was serving at the front of the shop, that John Turner came to the counter. I knew him from the Bull and Mouth meeting: a strong, well-set man of about thirty years who worked as a porter at Paul's Wharf – though he was often out of work now because of the plague.

"Will!" he exclaimed. He was breathless, and I realized he'd been running. "They've brought about fifty Friends – prisoners – out of Newgate! They're marching them down to the wharf at Blackfriars. We reckon they're to be transported at last."

"They've found a ship?" I turned to Agnes, who was near by. "Fetch thy father." She sped away.

"Seems so," said John. "Friends are gathering at Blackfriars. Come if you can. I'm spreading the word."

He hurried away. James appeared, with Agnes trotting alongside, full of the importance of her mission.

"I must go there," James said. "And you too, Will? Agnes will help mind the shop, won't thou, my good girl?"

He left Cecily in charge, and the two of us made our way to Blackfriars Wharf, where we found many Friends gathered, and a barge waiting.

Nat and his employer, Amos Bligh, were among the crowd.

"Nat!" I called. And when we reached each other I asked, "Is it true? They've found a captain?"

"They have. Fudge, his name is – master of the *Black Spread-Eagle*. Says he'd transport anyone, even his own family. The ship lies at Bugby's Hole. They will take the prisoners out to it on the barge."

A murmur ran through the crowd of waiting Friends. The prisoners were coming: a line of them, guarded by turnkeys and officers. As they passed, people came to their windows and out of shops to stare and jeer – more often at the prison officers than the prisoners. Most of the prisoners were men, but there were perhaps a score of women among them.

I recognized several people from our meeting – in particular a young man Nat and I had become friends with: Vincent Chaney, a silversmith, who had been in prison several months. I was shocked by his appearance. He'd always been a slight man, but now he was gaunt, with a straggling beard; dirty and defeated-looking. His wife, Rachel, broke suddenly from the crowd and flung herself towards him, crying out his name in such grief that the people in the shop doorway behind me tutted in sympathy, and a woman called out, "Let her say farewell to her man! Poor girl!"

Vincent turned, his eyes seeking Rachel.

But the officers seized her and pushed her roughly aside. She collided with Nat, who stood beside me, and he caught her and gave her into the care of her women friends, where she collapsed in uncontrollable weeping.

By now the prisoners were beginning to board the barge. Though they did nothing to resist, they held back and had to be forced and prodded aboard with a good deal of foul language, while the people around shouted at the officers. We Friends were mostly silent, although a few spoke out. Elizabeth Wright began to preach that the city was cursed for its wickedness. "Repent! Repent!" she cried. And Joseph Law fell to his knees in prayer on the cobbled road, and was kicked and beaten until he got up.

But at last all were aboard, and the barge was cast off and proceeded downriver. We stood and watched its progress until we could see no more – the ship's mooring at Bugby's Hole being far away, beyond Deptford Reach.

We all began to disperse, shocked and distressed, talking together.

James told Rachel Chaney he was hopeful. "They have yet to get them aboard ship," he said. "They may have found a master, but few seamen have much stomach for this work."

It turned out he was right, for next morning we heard that only four of the prisoners had been got aboard, and those with much difficulty, since they would not move themselves and must be dragged or carried. The master had been absent, and the seamen, despite threats and curses, had refused to help in any way. At last the officers had admitted defeat and brought the remaining prisoners back to Newgate. But we knew they would try again.

Two weeks later – on the first fourth-day in August – another day of prayer was ordered to be held throughout the city. My employer closed our shop, and we all went to the Bull and Mouth meeting, where we found Friends assembled in large numbers. We half feared an assault by the authorities, but there was none; perhaps even they were at prayer.

Nat was there; and Rachel Chaney with her child, a little girl of perhaps a year and a half; and some other younger Friends of our acquaintance: Mark Ashton, a carpenter; and Francis Palmer, who was servant to a notary.

When the meeting for worship was over, we talked about our Friends in Newgate. Edmund Ramsey, a city merchant who sometimes attended our meetings, had heard a rumour that the authorities would make another attempt to embark the prisoners on sixth-day – and that they would be better prepared this time, and send more officers.

"We must make a presence," said Joseph Law. "Pray, and exhort them, and give comfort to our Friends."

"I say we should hire boats," said John Turner. He'd know the boatmen, I realized, since he worked on the waterfront. "With boats we can follow the barge out to the ship, and be there with our Friends until the very last moment."

This was seized upon eagerly, especially by the wives and mothers of some of the prisoners.

Joseph Law agreed to spread the word among other meetings, and John Turner undertook to hire three boats for the twenty or so people from our meeting who wanted to go.

I had some anxiety about whether I should join them. I'd resolved to stay clear of trouble this year, if I could, so as to be sure of getting to Shropshire to marry Susanna. And yet, for the first time since our plans to leave London had been disrupted, I felt some excitement and enthusiasm. It would be a show of support for our Friends, but it would also carry an enticing edge of risk; and Nat was going, and all the other young men. I didn't want to be left behind with the elders. And it was not illegal to hire a boat. I said I'd go.

When the day came, my employer stayed to mind the shop, but I went, with his permission, down to the wharf at Blackfriars.

We waited till the prisoners were on the barge and it had been cast off before going aboard our own boats. Nat and I were in the smallest boat, along with John Turner, Rachel Chaney and two women Friends supporting her, Sarah Chandler and Rebecca Edge.

The day was warm, but as we moved out onto the river I felt the cool wind ruffling my clothes. Rachel was calmer today, her face pale and set. Nobody believed the prisoners could escape transportation now, so she must have known she would be seeing her husband probably for the last time.

The women sat with their arms around Rachel, and we three young men stood together at the other side of the boat. The boatman was an acquaintance of John's, a rough-spoken man with no patience for the workings of so-called justice. He provided a commentary on the idiocy of prison officers, turnkeys, judges and soldiers as we swung out into the current and followed the crowded barge.

Other small boats with more Friends aboard came out from the Southwark side, and more still as we passed the Tower. I began to feel exhilarated, as if we were setting off on an adventure; and I guessed the other two felt the same. Only the presence of the unhappy young woman restrained our spirits.

Then Rachel cried out, "God help us! Soldiers!"

From the Tower, we saw several boatloads of soldiers setting out. The sight of them in their red coats, with sunlight glinting on their muskets, struck alarm into me and – no doubt – deadly fear into Rachel. They had clearly been sent to make sure the prisoners were all got aboard this time.

As one of their boats drew closer a captain shouted to us to be gone.

"Turn back! We have orders to sink you if you obstruct us!"

I knew they'd have no mercy if we got in their way. The dirty Thames slapped at the sides of our boat, unpleasantly close. Sarah Chandler began to pray aloud, so that our Friends might hear, and the rest of us joined in.

The coarse jeers and laughter of the soldiers carried across the water.

"Canting dogs! Holy Joes! Be off!"

"And take your whores with you!"

"Drown the fools!"

We ignored the abuse. Our boatman began to swear in return, but Sarah laid a restraining hand on his arm and, with some reluctance, he fell silent.

Now our spirits rose. As we passed Horsleydown, and then Wapping, more and more little boats left the shore on either side; and we recognized in them the plain black hats and sober clothes of Friends. Meetings from all over London and Middlesex had members on the barge, and soon a small flotilla of boats followed in its wake and outnumbered the soldiers. The prisoners on the barge, seeing us all, must have felt supported; and I began to believe that by sheer weight of numbers and the power of prayer we might yet change the course of events.

And so we continued around the bend in the river and out beyond Deptford to Bugby's Hole.

When we saw the *Black Spread-Eagle* a cry of despair broke from Rachel. The ship was as grim as her name: painted in peeling black, and with a filthiness about her that could be seen even at this distance and that brought a foul smell towards us on the wind. No one knew what trade Fudge had been engaged in, but I felt, with an instinctive revulsion, that this might have been a slave ship – for I knew that English ships did engage in that evil trade; and Fudge was clearly a man without honour or human sympathy.

The barge had now come alongside the ship, and we heard the shouts and commands of prison officers and soldiers. The soldiers climbed swiftly aboard the barge. The prisoners were herded to the side, and the seamen, who had assembled on the deck of the *Black Spread-Eagle*, were commanded to assist.

Rachel stood up, craning to see her husband.

It soon became apparent that the seamen would not cooperate. They stood idle, and would neither prevent nor assist the operation. The master could be seen swearing and exhorting them to no avail. The prisoners, for their part, would not go willingly aboard. They did not resist, but let their bodies become limp, so that the soldiers and prison officers struggled to lift and move them. Meanwhile our flotilla of Friends' boats surrounded the scene, and we prayed aloud and called out words of encouragement.

The soldiers grew rougher. Some got aboard the ship. Others beat the prisoners with the butts of their muskets, forced them to the side and heaved them up and over the rail onto the ship, where they were seized by those aboard. The violence increased as the prisoners continued to fall limp to the deck rather than go meekly to their fates. People were dragged on board, buffeted and scraped against the bulwark and hurled onto the deck, where the master drove them below. Women were treated as roughly as men, and with deliberate disrespect. I saw one young woman pulled aboard upside down, her skirts over her head, the soldiers leering as her buttocks and thighs were exposed. A man was caught by one arm and leg, swung, and thrown down on top of her before she could rise.

There was wailing as well as prayer and encouragement from Friends aboard our little boats as many saw those they loved beaten, injured and degraded.

Rachel cried out when her husband appeared, dragged by his armpits to the edge of the barge.

He was dealt with quickly. A soldier heaved him up, and another on the *Black Spread-Eagle* hauled him on board backwards.

"Vincent!" Rachel screamed.

But in a moment he was gone, driven down into the hold of that foul ship.

Rachel turned a face of anguish to us. "It is a death ship. I shall never see him again."

The two women tried to comfort her. "Have faith, Rachel, have faith."

But I feared Rachel was right; and even if her husband did survive, it would be more than seven years before she saw him again. My own separation from Susanna was nothing by contrast.

It took over an hour to get the fifty or more prisoners aboard. Such violence had been used that we feared some of them could now be lying below with broken limbs.

At last all was done. The soldiers returned to their boats and sailed back to the Tower, the small boats full of Friends going to their various home wharves. Our three remaining boatloads followed the barge back to Blackfriars Wharf.

We were a subdued group as we came ashore and walked up towards Paul's Churchyard. The excitement and bravado had gone, and now we reflected on the cold reality of our Friends' fate. The prison officers from the barge were laughing and joking, jubilant at their success. One of them, swaggering past me, knocked my hat off into the gutter. As I stooped to retrieve it, he said, "Much good your praying did those fools!"

I should have ignored him, but the close contact with Rachel Chaney's grief had made me angry. I slammed my hat back on my head, and retorted, "It is you who are fools! Who turn away from Christ's mercy and send honest men to their deaths!"

The joviality vanished in an instant. Now the man was menacing. He stepped in front of me; forced me to stop.

"Do you call me a fool, sirrah?"

Friends and prison officers alike paused; I felt the tension in both groups, and saw Francis Palmer make a slight warning gesture.

I was frightened now. How had I got into this? It was nothing to me, their strutting and crowing; why had I responded to it?

I took a breath and said evenly, "I call on thee to attend to the light within."

"You call on *me*!"

He lunged forward, knocking me off balance. I moved to go past him, but he hit me again and I felt blood running from my nose. Francis came to my aid and was pulled away. I heard Nat shout my name;

he was down nearer the wharf, with the women, but he came hurrying up the street with other Friends as the officers surrounded me and two constables appeared. As they seized me I became aware of another scuffle close by and saw John Turner knocked down.

People on the street and leaning out of windows clamoured to be heard.

"They did no harm!"

"The turnkeys set upon them!"

But it made no difference. I was held, pinioned by the arms, and heard the constable's voice – "I arrest you on a charge of causing an affray" – and moments later three of us were in the custody of the prison officers, on our way to Newgate.

I turned, saw Nat struggling to reach me, the constables barring his way. I shook my head at him, mutely urging him to keep back.

I was bound for Newgate, along with my Friends John Turner and Francis Palmer, who might have been safely home by now if I had not spoken out. I felt guilt as well as despair. A few streets on I saw the familiar gateway. It always filled me with dread, but never more so than now. Inside, I knew, the plague had taken hold, and Friends were dying from it every day; buried in the common graveyard within the prison. I had not meant to come here this summer. I had been determined to keep myself out of prison, to be free to marry Susanna. Now I realized I might never see her again. I could pay for that moment of anger with my life.

Susanna

*A*fter Dan and Judith left Hemsbury, it seemed the summer yellowed and faded fast, and my spirits with it. I shall die a virgin, I thought; for sometimes I feared Will must be dead, and I could not imagine loving anyone else. I felt lonely without Judith; and my work, which used to be satisfying, was nothing to me now. I wrote to Will regularly, as I always had, and tried to write of things that would amuse or cheer him, trusting that he would somehow receive my letters. But news came from London of three thousand dead of the plague in one week; of pits being dug to accommodate the great increase of corpses; of rows of shops empty and grass growing in the streets. From Friends we heard of the deaths of many of our people, both in Newgate and in the city at large.

I scanned those lists, dreading to see Will's name. It was not there. Did that mean he was alive? I could not be sure, for London seemed to be a place where all order and communication was breaking down. Sometimes I lay awake at night, and then my darkest thoughts came to me. I imagined Will lying dead, tumbled into a plague pit. I knew I should think of death as a release from suffering and a joyous reunion with God, but I could not. I wanted my love here, now, with me on this earth, in our earthly bodies.

One day, when I was alone in the bookshop, the door opened, and Henry Heywood came in.

I stiffened with fear and my heart began to pound. This man was my enemy, the one who had tried to part Will and me; who had called me a whore and connived (so I believed) with Robert Danson to have me put in the stocks. Why had he come? He had never set foot in the shop before – or not since I'd been working here. Was he here to abuse me for having caused his son to go to London, into danger?

Or did he have news for me? Bad news? At that possibility I felt faint, and reached for the edge of the table to support myself.

He seemed agitated. He paced back and forth, then swivelled abruptly to face me. Without introduction, or any form of address, he said, "Have you heard from my son?"

I steadied my breathing. "No," I said. "Not since midsummer."

Did he know we were to be married, I wondered? Had Will told him? I remembered that Will had said his letters to his father were never answered, and I felt a surge of anger. If Henry Heywood wanted news of his son, why had he ignored him for so long? Why come troubling me in my unhappiness?

I regarded him stony-faced.

"You people have lists, I heard," he said. "Lists of … Quakers" – his voice broke on the word – "dead of the plague…"

I saw then that he feared Will was dead; and feared also that he was so far alienated from his son that he might not have been told. It was desperation that had driven him to speak to me.

"Will's name was not on any list," I said. "But I did hope to have heard from him, and have not."

His shoulders sagged.

"The post is perhaps disrupted," he said; but his voice sounded as bleak as my own feelings.

Until then I had thought of this man only as my tormentor; now I saw him as one who loved Will, and I knew how my own father would feel in such circumstances. A little of my fear left me, and was replaced by pity.

"If I hear any news," I said, "I will send to thee at once."

And pray do the same for me, my heart begged him, though I would not say the words.

He nodded – curtly, I thought – and strode to the door. As he reached it, he turned back and looked fully at me, as if seeing me for the first time.

For a moment, as he held my gaze, he seemed on the point of saying something more; then he opened the door and went out.

William

I remembered Newgate well.

We were taken to the common side, below street level, where the poorer sort are housed. As soon as we entered, a great hubbub hit us: hundreds of voices, shouting, swearing, screaming, arguing. The smell of the place rose up and enveloped us: a sour, fetid smell that made me catch my breath with fear and loathing. An army of bedbugs and lice inhabit the place; they crunched underfoot as we walked through. In Newgate the very walls seem impregnated with the sweat and suffering of all those who have been incarcerated here. Always, when I enter this place, I fear I will never leave it alive. In our meetings I have sought to find courage in the contemplation of Christ's suffering, for I know I must return again and again; yet the terror remains; I know I am not made of the stuff of martyrs.

All three of us were shackled in leg irons and shut into the same huge room, where perhaps a hundred people were imprisoned. As we arrived, a prison officer went through our clothing and removed our money: garnish, they call it. Like the others, I lost little, since I had not brought much more than my boat fare; but that only served to annoy those who had us in their power. This time, I soon realized, would be worse than before. The officer I had provoked – his name was Sadler – intended to make me suffer for my insult. He was a dark, thickset, brutal man, clever enough to be cruel. He beat me about the head and body till my ears rang and I was forced to curl up to protect myself. Then two of them seized me, hauled my arms above my head and, before I knew what was happening, fastened manacles around my wrists, chained to rings high up on the wall. I was left standing with my arms at full stretch.

"Leave him a few hours like that," Sadler said to the other. "Let him learn respect for the law."

I felt shock and fear as well as pain. I had been in prison before, but never had I been singled out for punishment. In this position I felt exposed, vulnerable to attack, and the strain in my shoulders began to tell immediately.

A prisoner sat near by, watching me, and puffing on a clay pipe. He was a little, weasel-faced man of no particular age who looked as much at home as if he'd been born here. "You're lucky," he said. "Tall. When I was in the irons I couldn't get my feet flat on the floor."

My two friends, Francis Palmer and John Turner, pleaded with our jailer to let me down, but the man told them he had orders to leave me there. "I don't argue with Mr Sadler," he said.

It was already late in the day; the time for supper was past, even had we money to pay for it, and we were hungry, having been on the river much of the day. Some prisoners were drinking beer; the sight of it made me thirsty. My arms ached; the manacles were beginning to cut into the base of each hand; it was difficult to breathe comfortably with my arms raised, and the room was thick with tobacco smoke. As the evening drew on, the prisoners began lighting candles. These were tallow, and smelled foul.

My two friends squatted on the floor close beside me and we fell silent and tried to shut out that vile place and turn our minds to Christ. I gazed at the light from one of the tallow candles, marvelling at how so crude a substance could produce such a pure flame; and I reflected that even the hardest of men, such as our jailers, must have somewhere within them a glimmer of the light. I held on to that thought.

While my mind was on the light I felt the manacles less, but after what seemed like several hours the pain increased. There was numbness in my wrists and hands, and my back and shoulders hurt; I tried to stretch and relieve the weight on my shoulders but could not. The thought that they might leave me like this all night threw me into a panic.

"Jailer!" I shouted. "Jailer, are you there? Let me down, I beg you! *Jailer!*"

John went to the door and called again on my behalf. No one came; but the other prisoners yelled abuse, much of it obscene.

Francis begged for some beer from another man, and brought it to me; and I sipped it gratefully but awkwardly, the liquid trickling down my chin.

And then at last came footsteps and jangling keys; the door opened, and there were Cecily Martell and Hannah Palmer, bringing bread, cheese and beer, blankets for us to lie on, and money to pay for food and candles.

"Oh, Will!" exclaimed Cecily. "How has thou come to this?" She rounded on the jailer. "You have him chained like a felon! He has done nothing to deserve this! Can he not be freed now it is night?"

Hannah, who is Francis's elder sister, added her

entreaties. But the turnkey grumbled and muttered about orders, and they were obliged to leave us after bidding me hold fast and trust in the Lord.

John fed me by lifting food to my mouth.

"We must eat now, without delay," he said quietly. "Otherwise the felons will steal the food from us."

I knew he was right, but it was difficult, and I ate little.

Soon after, another visitor came: John's wife, Rebecca, whom he had married before he joined the Friends of Truth. The two of them spoke together in low voices, the woman tearful and accusing, John trying to calm her. And although I could see that they were at odds with each other, yet I envied them their intimacy and wished I could have been married by now, as I'd intended, with a wife who cared enough to be angry with me.

When his wife had gone, John wrapped a blanket awkwardly around me to stave off the night chill, and asked me if there was anything else he could do to ease my pain. But there was nothing. The ache spread to my lower back and hips and I longed to fall to the floor and lie among the lice and cockroaches. John and Francis wrapped themselves in their blankets and lay down near me, but they were restless and I knew they slept little. When it grew late most of the candles were extinguished, but a few remained, casting shadows onto the faces of those who played dice, or drank, or talked the night away. One man, who seemed to be an idiot, sang and raved continually. Several fights broke out over sleeping places, and in the dead of night someone attacked Francis and tried to steal his blanket from under him; only the peaceful intervention of John, who had a strong, quiet presence, prevented it.

It was then, when the noise of that scuffle had died down, that I first heard screams and howling from somewhere within the building. The sounds were scarcely human. They made me shiver with fear.

Slowly a grey morning light showed in the barred openings near the ceiling. My mind was now exhausted, my eyes constantly closing and then jerking open again as the drop into sleep caused even more pain in my arms and shoulders. It became so unbearable that I groaned aloud and begged for someone to help me.

At last came the sound of keys; the jailer entered, and unlocked my manacles. I fell to the floor and crouched there, curled like a child and rubbing my bruise-blackened wrists, while tears trickled from under my closed eyelids. The numbness cleared and my blood began to flow again, but I trembled for hours. My friends comforted me and we kneeled among the lice and bugs and prayed together.

"Holy Joes!" we heard; then jeering laughter and, "You won't find God down here!"

"We're all going to the Devil – try praying to *him*!"

I shut my eyes and ignored them.

A commotion and sudden outburst of shouting startled me. At first I thought it was more mockery; then I heard a scream: "Plague! Plague!"

My eyes flew open in terror. A man had collapsed. He was sweating and groaning. A clear circle grew around him as everyone drew back.

"He has the signs!" Someone pointed. "See! In his neck!"

I saw a purplish swelling there.

People began yelling for the jailers. Two turnkeys came in, looked at the prostrate man, then seized him by the arms and feet and began to carry him away.

"His blanket!" a prisoner shouted.

No one wanted to touch the thing. It was kicked into a corner.

The weasel-faced man told me, "They have a room they take them to – the ones that get the plague."

I remembered the screaming I had heard in the night, and now realized, with horror, its significance.

"Does anyone attend to them?" I asked.

He shrugged. "No physician or apothecary would come in here."

I thought of those cries. I knew the sickness

caused headaches so severe and prolonged that people would beat their heads against the walls. The buboes – black swellings in the neck, armpit and groin – caused still more pain. Death, when it came, must be a mercy.

When Sadler appeared in the afternoon I tried to shrink back into the crowd; I feared I would be returned to the manacles. But instead we three and several other prisoners were taken out and marched to the courthouse next door, where the mayor was to hear our cases.

I was first. The charges against me were that I had congregated with others in the street in a riotous and unlawful manner, to the terror of the people, and in so doing had incited an affray.

I denied this, and said there was no unlawful congregation; that we were walking peacefully in the street.

"In a group of twenty or more?" the mayor said.

I knew it would not advance our cause to explain why so many of us had been there, so I merely repeated the truth, that we were walking to our homes.

I was found guilty of the offence and fined five pounds, which I refused to pay, and was therefore committed once again to Newgate for two months or until I should pay.

I thought of Susanna, of our plans to marry. Had

I been alone I might have been tempted to pay, and go free. But Friends never paid such fines on principle, and I knew John and Francis would be steadfast in the truth. They followed, gave similar responses, and were committed with me.

Now that he had us back in his power, Sadler continued to single the three of us out for punishment. He beat and ridiculed us, and forced us to lie in a place that was always damp from water seepage. Francis, who had never had strong health, developed a cough that he could not shake off.

Sadler took against me in particular – I think because he believed I set myself above him. James Martell would bring me in news-books with essays on philosophy and religion. On one occasion Sadler tore up one of these, declaring it to be lies and filth. I guessed he could not read and so resented me.

I was thankful, next day, that Sadler was not about when Nat came with a letter from Susanna. There was nothing I longed for more, and I snatched it from Nat in my eagerness. Later, I sat a little apart from John and Francis, and broke the seal and unfolded it. Susanna did not know where I was, or even if I was alive or dead, but she had continued to write to me all summer. Her letter reminded me that there was a happy, everyday life I might one day return to. She'd often made me laugh with tales of small disasters in the print shop, or the sayings of her friend Em; today it was the long-winded ramblings of one of our earnest Hemsbury Friends. I smiled as I read it, knowing him well.

John watched me fold the letter and tuck it inside my shirt.

"Thy girl?" he asked.

"Yes." I sighed. "We should have been married by now."

"This will end," he said. "Never fear."

Throughout our imprisonment, the bond grew between Francis, John and me. We took good care of each other. Francis was eighteen years old, one of a family who were all Friends of Truth. John had come to Friends by reason of his own inner searching and prayer. He was a strong but gentle man, who could read little but was never seen without a Bible. He was the wisest of the three of us, and knew how to reason with guards and violent prisoners without either antagonizing them or giving ground.

He took especial care of Francis, whose health had deteriorated, making sure he ate enough and was protected as much as possible from the damp. But Francis grew weaker. One day he woke restless and shivering, complaining of a fearsome headache. By evening he burned with fever.

John took me aside. "I fear it may be the plague.

We must do what we can for him – and pray."

We stayed close to Francis, caring for him, and hoping against all reason that John was wrong, until the buboes – proof of plague – were found, and the guards came to take him away. By this time the cell was in uproar and Francis was crying out in agony.

"Let us go with him!" John pleaded.

"No one except the sick is allowed in there." They shut the door on us.

"But he'll have no friend!" I shouted. "No one!" I beat on the door.

We never saw Francis again. Together we kneeled and prayed for him. His family came, his mother distraught and hardly able to stand, sobbing that she would go in and care for all those who were sick, his sister screaming as they refused her admission. But it was not allowed, and they left. I felt that Sadler took particular pleasure in thwarting Quakers.

Four days later we heard that Francis had died. I clung to John and sobbed. I knew Francis was now with Christ in Paradise, but that did not prevent me from being overcome with grief; the more so when his body was removed and buried in the prison pit even before his family had been informed.

The following night I noticed on John's forehead a film of sweat; and though it was a hot night I felt uneasy. I dared not speak to him or ask if he felt unwell, for fear of making it come true.

In the early morning I heard him shivering and groaning, and knew my fears were not unfounded.

"John," I whispered, "art thou sick?"

He turned to look at me, and in the half-light I saw the terror in his eyes: John, who had never shown fear of any man or any punishment.

"Pray for me – and for my poor wife," he said.

He asked me to read to him from Paul's letter to the Romans, and by flickering candlelight (for it was not yet full day) I read aloud: "'Who shall separate us from the love of Christ? Shall tribulation, or distress, or persecution…'"

There were rustlings and sighs around us. Someone snarled, "Let a man sleep, for Christ's sake!" But I was aware that others were listening, and I continued, more strongly than before. "'For I am persuaded, that neither death, nor life, nor angels, nor principalities, nor powers, nor things present, nor things to come, nor height, nor depth, nor any other creature, shall be able to separate us from the love of God, which is in Christ Jesus our Lord.'"

John nodded, and licked his dry lips. "It is the truth," he said.

Next morning he found the swellings in his armpit and groin, and the guards took him away from me. Later I heard, outside our door, the screams and raving of his wife when she was told, and the curses she threw upon jailers and Quakers alike.

"Fetch an apothecary!" she cried. "Mr Baynard in Coleman Street. He treated my cousin for the plague, and she lives! Fetch him!"

The sound of her cries retreated as she was hustled away. I felt shaken, and wretched. I knew she was right. At home, with her, and with the care of an apothecary, John might have a chance of recovery. Here he had none.

He died three days later. His wife shrieked as they took his body away, and I curled myself into a ball, with my hands over my ears, unable to bear it. Now I was alone, without friends in this place, overcome with grief and guilt. I blamed myself for the deaths of my two friends, believing they might never have been in Newgate if I had not spoken out that day at Blackfriars. I waited now for the sickness to claim me too, and felt sure it must.

The day John died all the bells in the city were silent. I had been scarcely aware of them, for their ringing had been an almost continuous sound with so many dying every day. It struck me strangely because of my distress, but later someone told me that an order had gone out that passing bells should no longer be tolled.

It was a week later, when my spirits were still low,

that I began to feel ill. My head ached; I felt cold and shivery, then burning hot. Both Francis and John had sickened in the same way. When I saw the fear in the eyes of those around me I knew I was not imagining my illness.

I clenched my teeth against the shivering that wracked me. I knew it must be the plague. I would die, as my friends had died. I prayed to God that I would leave this earth with Christian courage and acceptance, but feared I would not; and I felt bitter self-pity that I must die without ever seeing Susanna again.

The other prisoners demanded of the jailer that I be removed. "Search him! Search for the tokens!"

An old woman was sent to look me over – a dirty hag whose breath smelled of spirits. She found no swelling in my armpits or groin, and no sign of the rash they call the tokens.

"It is a fever or ague," she said. "Not plague."

The other prisoners still wanted me removed, especially when I began to vomit. I was so dizzy that I was forced to crawl on hands and knees to reach the communal pisspot and puke into it. Weasel-face shoved it closer to me. My tongue felt dry, and I craved sips of beer continually, but had hardly enough strength to hold the tankard.

After a few hours the fever cooled, and sweat

broke out all over my body. I felt well again, and next day was much recovered. I felt in my armpits and found no swelling; and there was no rash on my body. Perhaps the old woman was right, and it was not the plague. In my weakness and relief I wept.

The next day the sickness and fever returned, more violent than before. I guessed then that my illness was indeed an ague; I had seen boys at school suffer with it and knew that it would come and go every other day until it had run its course – or the victim died.

When Cecily Martell saw me she went home and returned soon after with a pad of linen which she laid on my burning forehead.

"It contains a spider, bruised in a cloth," she said. "It is recommended for the ague. I have a little book of remedies I often use for the children."

I found her attention soothing, but the spider did nothing to prevent the next onslaught of fever. Neither did the pipe of tobacco that Weasel-face gave me and which he assured me was a protection against all ills. I grew weaker with exhaustion as the days went by.

"We must get thee out of here," said James Martell.

"No! I will not pay – nor have others pay."

But the next day the fever returned again. I was

wretched, sick, and could not stand without fainting. James and Nat came – and dimly, through my dizziness and nausea, I was aware of them talking about me.

That evening, the jailer told me I was to be released. Nat came in and helped me to my feet, and I clung to my friend and felt tears running down my cheeks. But still I protested: "I won't have anyone pay."

"It's that or the burial pit in the yard, I reckon," Nat said brutally. "Thou won't last much longer here."

We passed outside the gates, if not into fresh air, at least into freedom. I should have been glad, but all I could think was that Francis and John had died in that place; and guilt for their deaths weighed upon me.

In the street a carriage waited. I was astonished when my friends led me to the door.

"Who...?"

"Edmund Ramsey," said James. "He has paid thy fine, and insists that thou go to his home where thou can be properly cared for."

"I scarcely know him..."

I brought Edmund Ramsey to mind. He had come to the Bull and Mouth meeting occasionally, and also to James's shop: a man about my father's age, a merchant, well-to-do and a collector of books – noticeable at our meetings where most people are craftsmen or shopkeepers.

"He is concerned for thy plight," said Nat.

I allowed the two of them to help me into the carriage. Nat got in with me. He'd deliver me, he said, then walk home.

I fell back against the padded seat, exhausted. I was aware of my filthy condition, but I did not ask where Edmund Ramsey lived, or who would care for me; the weakness was sweeping over me again, and by the time we arrived I was half fainting.

I remember little of my arrival, except an awareness of calm, comfortable surroundings; Nat and someone else helping me to bed; some soothing drink; clean sheets that smelled of lavender. After the endless racket of Newgate, Edmund Ramsey's house was a well of silence, and I slipped gratefully into its depths, and slept.

When I woke the fever had broken again; I was in a sweat, and felt refreshed. I lay with my eyes closed, and heard something I had not heard since I left my father's house: the sound of someone playing a virginal.

Susanna

To William Heywood,
at Thomas Corder's house in Creed Lane, London.
The twenty-fifth day of September 1665.

Dear heart,

I write this in the evening, after work, and try to
picture thee also in thy room in London, perhaps with
Nat, eating hot pies from Pudding Lane (for I
remember what thou told me of thy habits). As long as
I hold thy image in my mind I can believe thee safe and
in good health. I know thou dare not write to me. We
receive few letters now, and there are fewer travellers on
the road to bring us news; but we know the pestilence
still rages and has begun to spread into the country.

Yesterday was first-day. We met at John Callicott's house, and John spoke long and powerfully of London's suffering. I thought of thee, and wanted so much to be with thee that my throat closed up and I could not speak. Mary says, "No news is good news", and so I must trust and believe.

The weather continues warm, but the leaves are beginning to fall. I pray thou will come before winter and take me back with thee to London. I shall not fear plague or persecution if we are together.

Forgive me, love, for these sad thoughts. I shall write thee something merrier next time. I will tell thee of Em Taylor's wedding, which is to be held on the feast day they call Michaelmas; and I may have news from Isaac in Bristol.

I have been reading John Donne, and like well his sermons and the Holy Sonnets and find much light in them. I have found also a book of his love poems, and send thee this, which comforts me:

Let not thy divining heart
Forethink me any ill,
Destiny may take thy part,
And may thy fears fulfil;

But think that we
Are but turned aside to sleep;
They who one another keep
Alive, ne'er parted be.

Thy love,
Susanna Thorn

William

I had been at Edmund Ramsey's house for nearly three weeks or so when Susanna's letter arrived: a short, sad letter that made me feel desperate to get up at once and set off to comfort her and reassure her that I was alive and well. But in truth I was still far from well – unable to travel. And I dared not write; a letter must pass through many hands, and Edmund Ramsey had told me that more than eight thousand Londoners had died of the pestilence in the last week.

My recovery from the ague was slow. It seemed the fever was reluctant to loosen its grip on me and would ease for a while, only to return again as bad as ever, leaving me exhausted and in poor spirits. I remained for several weeks in my room, away from the main areas of Edmund Ramsey's house, cared for by him and his servants. Because I had been in contact with the plague in Newgate, I was kept as secluded as possible, and my only visitor was Nat. Edmund paid Nat my share of the rent at the Corders' so that I would be able to go back there when I was well. I was grateful that he had taken me in, and not left Nat with the burden and risk of attending to me in our lodgings; and glad to be spared Meg Corder with her well-meant but insanitary ways. Here, the Ramseys' physician visited and prescribed soothing herbs, which the servants prepared. It was easier, in such a large house as this seemed to be, to keep the sick clean and apart. The kitchen was well stocked and the servants did not go out more than was necessary into the infected air of the streets.

When I first arrived I'd had no idea of where the house was. My host told me later that we were in Throgmorton Street, not far from the Exchange, and that he lived, at present, alone except for the servants, his wife and children having gone, for their safety, to relations in Essex. I had never met his family. When I saw him at the Bull and Mouth meeting he had always been alone.

"I dare not bring them into danger from the authorities," he admitted. "I am newly come to Friends, only this past two years. I have attended several different meetings – most often the one in

Gracechurch Street, which is nearest. But my wife and daughters worship at home. I have such fear for them. It is hard, when there is a family to consider."

I told him about my own family, which it seemed I had lost for good. "That first evening," I said, "when I came from Newgate, I thought I heard someone playing a virginal."

"Ah." He gave a wry smile. "I have not yet severed myself entirely from my former life."

"It made me think of home," I said. "I miss music."

"Thou used to play?"

"Yes. We had a virginal."

"Then thou must try our instrument – when Dr Waterford releases thee from this room! I used to play often, but now I try to use that time in prayer and silence. I have talked to Friends – it's what most of them advise. But I cannot deny music to my girls. My eldest, Catherine, is especially accomplished and would be loath to give it up. Thou'll find sheet music of hers, if thou wish to play."

"Thou'rt kind," I said, wondering if he would prefer me to resist the temptation. I sank back on the pillows.

I loved the peace of Edmund Ramsey's house, his quiet but stimulating company, and the books he brought me from his library. We talked about religion, the laws against Dissenters, about London, trade, and travel. He had been to Venice in his youth, and worked in Antwerp and Brussels – as I might have done had I not rejected my father's plans for me. When I told him about Nicholas Barron, the silk merchant I should have been apprenticed to, he exclaimed, "But I know him well! He lives a few streets away. He's been hard hit by the effects of the pestilence. Foreign ports won't allow our ships to unload. We can only hope the sickness soon abates."

Although we talked frequently, I spent much of my time alone, reading, or sleeping. Edmund was often out of the house, or busy about his work. Sometimes, when I was free of the fever, I walked in the garden. An almond tree grew there, and there were beds of salad herbs, and rosemary and lavender. But I was not well enough to go out, even if it had been safe to do so. Few people went out, unless they must. I heard that there was grass growing in the street in Cheapside – a thing I found difficult to imagine. I felt anxious, adrift, cut off from my work and plans, and from Susanna.

In the distant reaches of the house I would hear voices, footsteps, the clatter of pots and pans. Nat came to see me every few days, though I sensed he did not come eagerly. He always looked a little ill at ease, as if he found the surroundings too grand for his comfort. He brought me letters, and news of the meeting. I had been there about a month when he told me that the *Black Spread-Eagle* had still not left London, and that plague had broken out on the ship.

"It's nearly eleven weeks since the prisoners went aboard," he said. "The women are allowed some freedom, but the men are kept below decks all the time. They can never stand upright. Friends are petitioning continually for their release."

"And Rachel?"

"She has the love of the meeting. As thou dost. We all pray for thy recovery."

I had a sense that he was holding something back.

"I must get strong again," I said. "Edmund tells me the plague has begun to retreat this last fortnight. People will return to the city and I'll be needed at the shop."

That look – of something withheld – had come into Nat's face again.

"What is it?" I asked. And fear clutched at me. "Susanna…?"

"Not Susanna," Nat said at once. He looked at me pityingly. "It is James Martell."

"James has the sickness?"

I realized then that Nat had not mentioned my employer for some time; and I, with my recurring fever and lethargy, had not thought to enquire of him.

"He has died," said Nat. "Cecily died first—"

"Cecily too?" A sense of horror and disbelief swept over me. "But – but the children? And the maid – Dorcas?"

"They are all dead. Ten days ago. I would have told thee, only we – the meeting – agreed to wait till thou wert stronger…"

He put an arm about my shoulders as I began to weep. I could imagine only too well the agony of the family's last days.

"The children?" I said. "Were they left? Did they die alone?"

"No one was ever alone. Cecily and James died first, then Dorcas. But Jane Catlin was there, and stayed with the children until the end."

Jane Catlin. A good woman, but not their mother. How Agnes and Stephen must have screamed for their mother! I tried not to think of it.

Nat was crying with me now. "I didn't want to tell thee yet. They are with God, Will; all of them. We must take comfort from that."

We sat in silence awhile.

It was not until the next day that the thought came to me that I had lost not only my friend but my employment and future prospects. I had no work to return to. How could I offer marriage to Susanna now? I was little better off than when I had left Hemsbury.

I must write, I thought, as soon as it's safe. Air the letter well over vinegar and take all precautions. Tell her everything. And yet I dreaded the thought of writing down all the trouble that had befallen us; it would be a catalogue of horrors. A short letter must suffice.

Susanna

t last, about the time of the
feast folk call All Hallows, came a letter from Will.

When I saw his handwriting, I felt such relief and
happiness that I could not break the seal fast enough.
The letter trembled in my hands.

It was brief, written in a shaky script that frightened
me more than any news it contained. He had been in
prison, he said, and had been left weak from an ague
which would not let go of him; but not to fear – he was
recovering and being cared for by Friends.

*Such terrible things have happened, more than I
have strength or courage to tell thee now; only that
my circumstances are quite changed. I will write
thee more when I am able. Till then, dear love,
I pray God keep thee safe…*

This letter left me with more questions than answers. I scanned it again and again. How ill was he? Was he out of danger? What terrible events had occurred? What change? And when would I see him? He'd said nothing of our marriage, nothing of coming to Shropshire, nor of whether the ban on travel had been lifted.

I remembered my promise to Henry Heywood, and sent Antony with a note. It said simply that Will was alive and had written to me; and I received a brief acknowledgement in reply.

A few days later Mary had a letter from Nat which reassured us that both he and Will were safe. Nat was never one for long letters, but this was briefer than most and hinted, like Will's, at more news to come. A great fear began to grow in me that something had happened to prevent my marriage to Will.

At our next meeting for worship we heard that those London Friends sentenced to transportation were still on the prison ship, the *Black Spread-Eagle*, holed up at Woolwich, unable to sail because the master had been arrested for debt. The pestilence had come among them, and was taking their lives one by one. Despite the plague, it seemed, the persecution of our people in the city continued. Many of them suffered also from the loss of their livelihood – for almost nothing could be exported, seamen and porters were out of work, and the trade in goods such as wigs and used clothes had ceased almost entirely. Alice Betts, a shoemaker's widow and a woman of much simplicity and goodness, said she felt a concern to go to London and visit our Friends in that afflicted city.

That night I came to a decision. I could not live with my fears any longer. Since news had not come to me, I must seek it myself. I would go to London and find out what had happened to Will. As soon as I had made this decision, hope sprang up again in my heart. I began to believe that all would be well, as Judith had said.

I knew all manner of sensible arguments would be used by friends and family to keep me at home, but I resolved then and there not to listen to them. I'd travel with Alice Betts, if she'd have me; I reckoned I'd find an ally in her. I had told Will, long ago, that when the time was right I would go to him; that no one should prevent me. I believed that time had come now.

William

owards the end of October the Ramseys' physician decided I was no longer a plague risk, and Edmund allowed me out of my confinement. It was a great joy for me to be able to join him that evening at dinner and to feel that I had re-entered the world. When I went into prison it had been full summer. Now the leaves of the almond tree in the garden were yellow and falling; winter would soon be here.

I was still alone most days, since Edmund was out and about with his business, but now I had access to other parts of the house. It was a much grander establishment than my father's, where we lived over the warehouse, and yet Edmund Ramsey was a merchant like my father, if a wealthier one, and the way of life was familiar to me. My father had his closet with a globe and maps and several shelves of books; but here there was a library – a room filled from floor to ceiling with books of all kinds. In the drawing room were gilt-framed mirrors, oriental vases, a small cabinet inlaid in ivory with birds and flowers, polished wood underfoot. Also in that room was the virginal: a pretty instrument painted with landscape scenes; my sister would have loved it, I thought, and I felt a stirring of homesickness.

Music had left my life almost completely since I became a Friend. I still had the flute I'd brought with me from Shropshire, and sometimes, at home with Nat, I would play a few tunes; but most Friends had come to disapprove of music-making, so there was no place for it in our social lives.

However, Edmund had said I might play if I wished. I opened the lid of the virginal, revealing another rural scene painted on the inside. There was sheet music on a low table near by. I leafed through it, noting several songs, a book of dances, but mostly instrumental music. I chose a piece by Byrd, one I knew from my schooldays at Oxford.

I began to play – and almost at once stopped. The stiffness of my fingers after so many years of disuse was unendurable. I flexed and stretched them, and tried again.

Still my performance did not please me, though

a little of the stiffness gradually wore off. But Byrd's music woke in me memories of playing the harpsichord and flute at school in Oxford, and of singing in the church choir. A whole world had been closed to me since I turned my back on the Anglican Church. I found myself longing for my father's house, for the music we used to play, the songs and rounds we'd sing together.

I played on, absorbed in the music, and felt the horrors of Newgate begin, at last, to fall away from me. Surely, I thought, a world in which such beauty existed could not be lost to God?

That evening, as we sat in the dining room, I thanked Edmund for his kindness and for the solace the music had brought me.

"But I must find work," I said. "I have imposed on thy generosity for too long."

"Thou might work for *me* for a while, if thou wish," he replied.

"For thee?" I was surprised.

"Not in my business. Here, in my library." Evidently this was something he had been considering. "I wish to sort and catalogue the books; remove some I no longer think suitable since coming to Friends; reorganize the remainder. Thou could help. It would provide some small paid employment for thee for a few weeks – if thou'rt willing."

It sounded congenial work, of a kind I was accustomed to. And yet... "I am more than willing," I said, "but I should do it as payment for thy hospitality."

We were dining on excellent beef and drinking Rhenish wine.

"Will, thou need'st money – and I need help." He smiled. "I shall not overpay thee, never fear."

"Then I would be glad to do it. Only ... thou'll remember I told thee I was to have been married this summer? I need to find permanent work, an income, a home..."

He nodded. "I understand. But because so many businesses are closed, there is not much work to be had. And thou'rt not strong enough yet."

I knew he was right. I had eaten scarcely anything for weeks; my clothes were loose on me, and my face in the mirror that morning had looked gaunt. But I could walk and take fresh air and begin to regain my strength. The colder weather had caused a steep drop in deaths from plague; it was considered safer now to go about the streets.

"Stay here, and work for me for a short while," Edmund suggested, "and in the meantime look about for other employment. My family are to come home on sixth-day. They'll be young company for thee. I wish, having taken themselves to safety, they would remain there somewhat longer, but my wife is anxious to return."

And so I stayed. I missed Nat's easy companionship, and yet it was a pleasure to be living once again in the sort of home in which I had grown up. The library work absorbed what little physical energy I had. The combination of lifting, climbing steps to the top shelves and moving armfuls of books from one place to another made me breathless at first, but in a day or two I was able to do it without difficulty. I also went out into the streets and saw how sadly empty they were: rows of shops still closed, and the Exchange with only a scattering of customers, very few of them gentry. I walked almost as far as Paul's Churchyard, but stopped short, and retraced my steps. It was not so much physical weakness: I could not bear, yet, to go there and see James Martell's closed-up shop. It would make the Martells' deaths too real. I still found it hard to believe that I would never see any of them again. For the same reason I had not yet written more fully to Susanna; that, and the feeling that I was now without prospects and had little to recommend me as a husband. I would write to her when I found permanent employment, I decided; then I could begin, at least, with some good news.

When the Ramsey family returned I was at work in

the library. I heard the coach arrive, the sudden clamour of voices, a dog barking, and felt a draught through the house as the side door was flung open and the servants brought in bags and boxes. The voices spread around the house; footsteps creaked on the floorboards of the room overhead; doors opened and shut. I did not venture out, being unsure of my status here. But at last I heard everyone gathering in the region of the drawing room, and then Edmund opened the library door and said, "Come and meet my family."

The drawing room seemed full of billowing silk skirts. With the mother were three girls aged between about twelve and seventeen. All were blue-eyed, fair and comely, though the youngest had been somewhat scarred by smallpox. Their little dog, a terrier, ran and barked at me, and the youngest girl stifled a giggle as she caught and subdued it.

Her father introduced them all. "My wife, Margaret; my daughters, Catherine, Jane and Dorothy."

"Thou'rt welcome, Will," said Margaret Ramsey.

I thanked her, and saw her taking in my appearance (shabby, I feared), my thinness, my way of speaking. I also felt her daughters' covert glances at me. The servants brought in spiced wine to warm the travellers, and Edmund invited me to sit down and join them. The girls sat in silence, upright and stiff in their boned bodices. Although they wore nothing ostentatious, they were richly dressed in silk gowns and their hair was bunched at the sides in curls in the current fashion, their caps arranged to display it to advantage.

Margaret Ramsey enquired politely after my health, and listened with pity in her face when I told her of the deaths of the Martell family. She asked about my own family in Shropshire, and I explained that I was estranged from my father. As I spoke I could not help but be aware of the eldest girl, Catherine, listening and watching me from under her lowered gaze.

"It is a great pity when religion divides a family," said Margaret Ramsey.

I knew her husband had become convinced of the truth only recently. She seemed to share his conviction – perhaps she felt that was her duty as his wife – but what had the girls thought about the changes this had brought to their lives? I had no chance that day to find out, for the supper which followed was a quiet meal, preceded by a silent wait upon God; and, in the manner of Friends, we spoke little.

I spent the following day in the library, as usual. I was determined to please Edmund Ramsey, and worked hard, making lists of all the books in the various categories. He owned many old and valuable books, some in French or Latin; also Camden, Holinshed, Hobbes, Robert Boyle, the Greeks and Romans. Most were bound in fine leather, the titles and decoration embossed in gold leaf, and the edges of the pages finished in gold. I came upon Plutarch, and remembered, with a pang of sorrow, Agnes Martell. "I shall learn to read it," she had said, imagining a future that would never be.

Edmund had asked me to put to one side any plays, anything that smacked of popery or superstition, anything I was doubtful about. I glanced at the plays: by Middleton, Shakespeare, Webster, Rowley. I sat on the floor some while, engrossed in a tale of two young lovers, parted by their warring families. I had never been to a playhouse, although when I was a child we had watched travelling players and enjoyed their performances. But play-acting was untruth – and certainly playhouses were known to be bawdy places, full of lewd jokes, the actresses whores.

I put *Romeo and Juliet* on the pile to be removed, along with Rowley's *All's Lost by Lust*.

The afternoon light was fading, and I began to think of finishing for the day. From the drawing room, below, I heard the sound of someone playing the virginal: awkward, stilted playing – young Dorothy, I guessed. The sound, mercifully, stopped; and then someone else took over. This time the music

– a country dance tune – was light and sprightly, perfectly judged.

I left the library and went downstairs to the landing, where a maid was lighting a candle in a sconce on the wall.

The drawing-room door was open. I stood in the entrance and saw that the player was Catherine. She was absorbed in the music, her hands sure and quick, blonde ringlets bouncing gently against her cheek.

The other two were dancing. They had joined hands and were tripping down the length of the room.

Catherine finished with a flourish, looked up, and saw me.

"Thou play well," I said.

She blushed. "It's a simple piece."

Her sisters stood pink and breathless.

"Play a jig, Kate," said Dorothy.

"Oh, Dorothy! Thou know Father does not like us to dance."

"But he's not home yet."

"I shall play a pavane. That is more seemly." She turned to me. "Would thou like to play something, Will?"

"I'll hear thy pavane first."

She began to play. "Look through the music on the table, there."

The stately sound of the pavane subdued her sisters, who danced gravely, like court ladies.

Before long their mother came in.

"Enough of this now, girls," she said. "You had your fill of dancing, I should think, at your cousins' house." She turned to me. "I'm sure you don't dance, Will?"

"Not any more."

"And don't approve?"

"I ... don't think about it a great deal." I hoped this was diplomatic.

She smiled, and I saw her daughters' prettiness in her face. "It creates laughter and exercise, which is innocent enough, I believe; but too much of it leads to frivolous thoughts, and to licence."

"I have no opportunity to dance," I said, "but I love music – and I have a flute that I play sometimes. It's good to keep in practice."

"Oh, yes!" agreed Catherine warmly – and blushed as she caught her mother's eye.

After her mother had gone out, Catherine said to me, "We used to play and sing every evening before Father was led to the truth. Our cousins in Essex are not Friends and it was like old times."

"Mother enjoyed it too," remarked Jane.

I felt pulled by different factions in the family and said, "Perhaps I should leave you…"

"No. Play for us," said Catherine. "Mother will not mind at all if it is something instrumental."

I found a piece by Orlando Gibbons.

Catherine stood up and let me take her place. The seat was warm from her body, and I was aware of her closeness as she stood beside me. She turned the pages, and the other two drew near.

As I finished the piece, Catherine said, "Thou hast grown up with music."

"Yes."

"And miss it?" She was looking at me with sympathy.

"More than I'd realized. But thy parents? Have they both given it up?"

"Almost. I think Father feels the loss greatly, but that only makes him more certain that he should resist it."

"Because it is a distraction?"

"Yes. He doesn't forbid *us* to play, but he doesn't like it to take up too much of our time. He believes we will give it up ourselves when we are ready."

"And will thou?"

I spoke teasingly, and was rewarded with a smile.

"I know I should hope so."

The next day was first-day. The family did not go out to Meeting, but gathered in their own dining room,

joined by two of their servants and six neighbouring Friends, among them the physician who had
attended to me, and his wife and brother. Since the
law allowed for only five to meet in addition to the
household, we were now an illegal meeting. I found
it difficult to see it as such, for here there was none
of the tension and excitement of a large meeting like
that at the Bull and Mouth, where one after another
would stand up to preach, and which was constantly
under siege. It seemed unlikely, unless Edmund
Ramsey caused trouble for the authorities, that his
house would be targeted.

The silence was deep, and I felt its intensity, and
afterwards marvelled that such power could be cre-
ated between so few people. I remarked on this to
Catherine as we left, and asked her, "Did you go
to Meeting in Essex?"

"No." She glanced up at me shyly. She had a
demure manner, not like Susanna with her straight
gaze. "We went to church with Uncle and Aunt and
the cousins. Mother would not seek out Friends with
Father not there."

"And which dost thou prefer?" For it was clear
that she had not yet chosen for herself.

"Church is easier," she said. "It's expected of us.
And more sociable – all society is there. And at St
Leonard's they have a good minister – his sermons

are not dull, like some. But I have never been to an outside Friends' meeting such as thou go to. Father forbids it because I am old enough now to be sent to prison."

She looked, I thought, so fair and vulnerable that it was no wonder he felt protective. I could not imagine such a girl in Newgate.

She, in turn, was looking at me.

"I can see thou hast suffered in prison," she said. "We must take care of thee."

Her mother had drawn near, no doubt mindful of her daughter's honour.

"Do many merchants or gentry attend meetings?" I asked, including the mother in my question.

"Very few," said Margaret. "There is Sir William Penn's son – also William; he must be thy age, Will, twenty or twenty-one. My husband met him once at Gracechurch Street last winter and believes it will not be long before he is convinced. A great trial to his father, who cannot tolerate his closeness to Friends; but a most vital and energetic young man... Now, girls" – she turned to gather the attention of her daughters – "no music today. Reading and sewing only."

We spent the rest of the day quietly. In the afternoon the women read the Bible and sat silently together, while Edmund and I went to the meeting at the Bull and Mouth. I arrived tired, for I still lacked strength, but was received with joy by my friends, most of whom had not seen me since I was sent to Newgate. It was a sad embrace I had with Hannah Palmer. All her youth and vigour seemed to have left her since her brother's death, and I was filled with renewed grief for Francis and for John Turner.

Jane Catlin tut-tutted at my hollow cheeks, but Nat asked me, "Will thou be going to Hemsbury soon?"

"Not yet. I've no work – nothing to offer Susanna. I'd be ashamed to face her father now. And thee?"

He shook his head. "Winter travel is hard. And I lost pay at the height of the plague. I'll go in the spring, maybe." He glanced across at Edmund, who was talking to some of the elders, and I thought I detected some feeling of rejection as he remarked, "Thou'rt settled in at Throgmorton Street, then? Seen the last of Creed Lane?"

"I'll come back soon – for a while."

I felt unclear about my future. When *would* Susanna and I be married? When we were, we'd need to find somewhere for the two of us to live. I remembered how excited I had felt about that, back in the spring. But now, everything had changed.

Susanna

"*I* still say thou'rt over-hasty," Mary said, opening the box in which she kept the print-shop money. "Thou might pass him on the road."

That gave me a moment's anxiety. But I knew the wording of his letter by heart; I had read it so often. There was no hint in it that he planned to come to Hemsbury: only that he'd write again when he was able; and he had not written.

"It's my chance to go with Friends," I said, "before winter sets in."

The thought of a winter of waiting was unbearable to me.

Mary counted the coins into my hand. They made up my final wages. Whatever I found in London, my life was about to change. I did not expect ever to work for Mary again. She knew that.

She looked at me, and sighed. "Thou'll be a loss to the business," she said, "and to me."

For a moment I thought she was about to embrace me, but then she patted my arm and said brusquely, "Well, put that away somewhere safe. Thou'rt off to see thy parents now, I suppose?"

"Yes."

Everything was arranged for the journey to London. Several others had joined Alice Betts in her concern to visit Friends in the city, and we were now a group of eight. Collections had been made at meetings around the county for the relief of distressed London Friends; we'd take the money with us, along with what spiritual comfort we could offer. Alice and I were the only women in the group. She was pleased to have my company and understood entirely my need to go, for she is a woman who always acts promptly on what seems right to her.

Back home, in Long Aston, I found my parents anxious about the plague and the dangers of the great city. My mother, especially, feared that I might find myself alone and heartbroken in London if – God forbid, as she said – something had happened to prevent my marriage to Will. But she understood my haste.

"He is ill, and has suffered," she said. "If I were in thy place, I would go to him straight away."

My father wanted to give me some money.

"I have my savings!" I protested. "Three years' worth."

"Then keep it well hidden under thy clothes."

"I shall, never fear. I'll wear layers of skirts in this cold weather."

He insisted on giving me extra for the journey. "London will cost you much," he said.

My mother brought out the wedding shift they had made for me.

"I'll come back, Mam," I said, "if I'm to be wed."

"Who knows what thou'll do? Take it now. London folk dress finer than us, I reckon. Thou won't want to look drab."

My father murmured against vanity, but my mother insisted, "'Tisn't vanity to be clean and comely."

And she hugged me hard, and said, "God bless thee, daughter, and help thee find thy love."

William

Over the next two weeks I grew rapidly stronger and put back the weight I had lost. The Ramseys made sure I ate well and did not work too long indoors, and I walked about the city and over to Westminster and Southwark on errands for Edmund to build up my strength.

My spirits also revived, and I began to feel again a sense of confidence in the future. I wrote to Susanna on the fifteenth of November, telling her not only of the help I'd had from Edmund Ramsey but about my time in prison; about the deaths of my friends and the responsibility I felt for them. I told her, too, of the deaths of the Martell family.

I am in no position, now, to offer thee marriage,
and yet there is nothing I desire more. I intend to

find a new employer and begin again. As soon as
I am settled and can find a home for us, I'll come,
or send for thee. It may mean a winter apart, but I
can't bring thee here, yet, to live in poverty in this
stricken city. Will thou wait for me, love? Tell me
thou will. I long for us to be together.

The weather was now cold, and the plague in retreat. People were returning to London in large numbers, and I knew that once the shops and businesses began to open again my chances of finding work would increase. Edmund made enquiries for me. Meanwhile I continued to sort and catalogue his books.

The Ramsey girls were always around the house, and we fell into a habit, in the late afternoon, of playing music together. The younger girls liked best to romp and sing – they treated me, I think, like a replacement for their merry Essex cousins – but Catherine had a true love of music, and the two of us enjoyed talking about it, and finding new pieces to play.

The three girls were educated at home by a tutor, though the plague had put a stop to their lessons for the time being. Catherine knew Latin, French, and some Greek and Italian. Sometimes we played and sang from a book of French songs she'd brought with her from Essex – light pieces, often about *"l'amour"*. I was aware of the danger of seeming to flirt with her

– for she had a shyness about her that invited it, and singing together caused us to exchange glances and smiles. I never spoke to her about Susanna – my love for Susanna was a private thing to me – but I felt sure her mother must have warned her that I was promised to another girl. This lay between us, unspoken, but I think we both knew that if it had not been for Susanna we might have drawn closer. As it was, I was careful to be no more than friendly, and to include her sisters in our conversations; and the mother kept a watchful eye on us all.

But Catherine was pretty and alluring – and she was there, and Susanna was not. I could not help feeling some desire for her.

It's innocent enough, I thought. And I'll be gone soon.

Susanna

We were to travel by carrier, probably in a cart open to the weather. I planned to wear a hat and hood, a heavy quilted petticoat under my skirt, and a large woollen cloak. In my bag I packed three shifts (two plain ones and my wedding shift), two collars, a few pairs of stockings, an extra woollen skirt and bodice, and a Bible. It seemed a fair-sized bagful, and the cloak was bulky. Alice took less: little more than she stood up in. She said, "'Consider the lilies of the field'," and directed me to Matthew's gospel. But I cannot bear dirty linen, so I took nothing out.

Right up to the last moment I hoped another letter would come from Will; but it did not. And so, on seventh-day the eleventh of November, Alice and I joined six Shropshire Friends in the yard of the

White Lion in Broad Street. A few other people were waiting, bound for Birmingham, or Coventry, but no others for London.

The carrier had a pack-train with horses and several carts. We were fitted in among bales of woollen cloth and sat on benches in reasonable comfort. The first overnight stop was at Shifnal. We rose early next day and joined local Friends at Meeting – for the carrier left later than usual on first-day mornings.

Having been only one day on the road it was irksome to me to have to stop at all, and I began the meeting in a state of restlessness, but Alice's testimony helped me to cease fretting and attend to the light within. She spoke simply of our group's mission and of the suffering of Londoners. She is a woman of some forty-five years, small and round and sweet-faced, very plainly dressed, and uncaring of her appearance – for her mind is turned continually to God. There is such gentleness about her that even those who despise Dissenters cannot help but respond to it.

Alice understood my anxiety to be away, and when at last we set off again she smiled and said, "Now, with God's grace to speed us, we shall go all the faster." But I confess I saw little evidence of it. The horses ambled on, and the carts bumped their way slowly over cobbles in town or ruts on the country roads; and once our cart slipped half into a ditch and had to be hauled out with the help of some men working in nearby fields. One of them winked at me as I stood waiting and seemed surprised when I did not blush or look away.

"Her gave me a straight look!" he joked to his companion.

His accent was strange to me. I wondered where we were, and how far on our way. In Mary's shop, before I left, I had spread out maps and looked at the route we might take, from Birmingham perhaps to Northampton, or Stratford, coming in to London from the north-west. I had travelled long distance before: to Oxford, to see Will; and when I was five or six years old I had moved from Bristol to Shropshire with my parents. But neither journey was as far as London.

Once back on the road, we travelled between endless fields, some full of sheep or cattle, some with men ploughing. For mile after mile the countryside looked much the same: brown fields, grey skies, flocks of birds following the plough. We passed through many villages about the size of Long Aston, and many small towns. Each night we stopped at an inn. Sometimes by the time we arrived I was so stiff and cold I did not enquire where we were, or care: only that there was a bed, and water to wash in, and a hot supper.

For several days it rained relentlessly, and our progress was slowed even more as the wheels churned through mud. The goods were protected under a layer of waxed cloth, and the carrier's men used some more of this to erect a rough shelter for us. From beneath it we peered out over the horses' heads at a dark, wintry world; some days it barely grew light.

I remember reaching Northampton, and Bedford, where new travellers came aboard; and then, after more than a week on the road, we reached Islington, our last overnight stop. I gazed across the fields in the direction of London and saw, less than two miles distant, the smoke from many fires, and what seemed to be a great flock of birds circling. Another traveller told us these were the kites which hung constantly above London, the middens and ditches being so plentiful that they were never short of carrion, especially in this time of plague.

Islington was a small village, but busy with many coaches and pack-trains. The inn where we stayed was full of travellers from all parts of the country; I had never heard so many different accents.

Next morning I woke long before dawn, and could not get back to sleep, my mind was so busy. I knew we'd be in London within a few hours – in the city itself, which Will had told me was little over a mile square. He'd be near; in no time, surely, I'd see him again. I tried to bring his face clearly to mind: his smile; his eyes, which I thought so beautiful – light greenish-grey, with dark lashes. I had no doubt that I'd know him, even from a distance. But his last letter troubled me: that shaky handwriting telling of changed circumstances. Anxiety mixed with my excitement.

At dawn we climbed aboard the cart for the last time. The sun was a pink glow in the east, the fields white with frost. Cold air stung my face, enlivening me. It would be a bright day.

The carrier set us down at Aldersgate.

The street was crowded and full of noise: wheels on cobbles, hawkers shouting, the harsh, fast speech of Londoners. I looked up and saw a great statue of a king on horseback atop the central arch of the gateway and other carved figures decorating the side towers. A woman carrying baskets of fruit and herbs bumped into me as I stood staring.

"Step aside, wench!" she said. "You block the way."

We gathered our group together and turned to walk into the city; and at once I saw ahead of us, rising above the shops and houses, a great steeple-house – so huge it could only be Paul's. It was a commanding slab of a building with a square tower covered in scaffolding. (God had struck off its steeple during a thunderstorm years ago, a Friend told me.) This vast steeple-house was to me a symbol of the power of the Church and its corruption. And yet my spirits rose when I saw it. I knew that Creed Lane, where Will lived, must be close by, and that he worked in a shop in Paul's Churchyard, and might be there at that very moment, so close I could reach him in minutes. I gabbled all this to Alice, and she said, "Child! Child! Be calm! We will find this inn our fellow travellers spoke of, and unburden ourselves, and give thanks to God for a safe journey. And then we will make enquiries."

We'd planned to stay at an inn the first night or two. Our group had names of Friends in the city, and we had no doubt that hospitality would be offered us once we had made contact with the meetings.

The eight of us split up and went to various inns near by. Alice and I found one that the carrier had recommended: the Three Tuns in Martin's Lane. A serving man showed us to our room, and set the luggage down; and then a girl brought us water for washing, and a mug each of small beer.

As I drank mine I looked out of the window into the street below, and saw crowds of people passing by – and yet the girl had said the town was half empty. A cart, laden with barrels, turned into the lane, its iron-shod wheels clattering over the cobbles.

A coach coming in the other direction blocked its way and the two drivers shouted at each other and made obscene gestures. The noise in the street, from voices, traffic, and goods being unloaded, was greater than anything I'd known in Hemsbury. The street was narrow, and the room we stood in was jettied so that it overhung the street. Below our window swung the inn sign, with its three barrels; other signs, painted on boards or hanging from poles, showed all the way along. I peered out, noting a glover's shop, and a saddler's. A hooded figure went by carrying a white staff, and I saw how the mass of people parted around this person, like water around an island, and none came near. An apothecary, I supposed, or a searcher: some such that dealt with plague sufferers. I shivered.

"Pull the window to," said Alice. "Let's give thanks."

So we sat down – Alice on the only chair, me on the bed. I closed my eyes and let myself become quiet and calm. I was here, and thanked God for it.

We remained silent for a few minutes. When I heard a slight movement from Alice I opened my eyes. She said, "Now I think we must eat."

I'd had nothing but a piece of bread since waking at Islington, and realized I was hungry. But first I wanted to be clean. I made Alice wait while I washed all over, and changed into clean linen and stockings, and combed my hair and set my cap neatly over it. There was a mirror on the washstand, and while Alice was occupied in reading her Bible I studied my reflection. I'd had no mirror in my room at Mary Faulkner's, so this was a novelty to me. I pulled out a strand of hair to curl either side of my face.

We ate in the main room of the inn, where I listened to the medley of voices around us. Londoners talk fast and clipped, and speak as if everything must be done today, and as quickly as possible. We attracted a few glances when we came in – I suppose because of our country dress – but we sat in a secluded corner and spoke quietly together.

A serving girl brought our meat. She was about my own age and wore a crimson dress, immodestly low-necked, I thought, and made of some fine silken material; I guessed it to be a rich woman's cast-off, for I had heard that there was a brisk trade in such clothes at city markets.

I asked her, "Dost thou know Creed Lane?"

She smiled a little at my slow way of speaking, and repeated, "Creed Lane? Yes! It's but a step away – the other side of St Paul's." And she described how to get there, so quickly I could hardly take it in, but reckoned I'd find my way. I had memorized Will's address: Thomas Corder's house, next to the Blue Boar.

"I thank thee," I said, as the girl left.

"I see nothing will hold thee now," said Alice.

"Will thou come?" I didn't want her to.

"No. I shall read my Bible, and wash, and perhaps sleep a little before taking the air. We shall meet later. Go carefully, Friend Susanna."

"I will."

I soon found Creed Lane. It was a short, steep road, and the Blue Boar lay at the bottom. On one side of it was a small shop, shuttered and locked, on the other a tall, narrow, run-down house where a woman in a dirty apron was swilling a bucket of food scraps into the gutter.

I asked her if this was Thomas Corder's house.

"It is." She regarded me curiously.

"I am looking for William Heywood." My heart beat fast as I spoke his name.

"Oh – Mr Heywood! You must ask Mr Lacon about him. He's at work."

"Who? Nat – Mr Lacon?"

"Yes. He works for a printer in Alum Court. He should be home in an hour. Do you want to come in and wait?"

I didn't. "I'll find him," I said.

"Other side of St Paul's. Off Old Change."

I thanked her and left.

Alum Court was near, but I struggled to find it in

the maze of busy streets where people crowded and jostled me, and where I had to crane my neck to look up at the signs. On the way I passed Paul's Churchyard, but many of the bookshops there were closed; and besides, the woman hadn't said Will would be at work; she'd said I must ask Nat. My anxiety returned.

At last I turned a corner into Alum Court – and there was the printer's shop, with the sign of the hand and pen, like Mary's, and the name *Amos Bligh* above it. The drop-down counter that opened onto the street carried a stock of quills and ink and various kinds of notebook. A youth minded it. I caught his eye and asked, "Is Nathaniel Lacon within?"

The boy called his name. And then Nat came out of the back of the shop, looking just as I remembered him: young for his age, ink-stained, fair hair hanging in untidy curls. He knew me at once.

"Susanna!" he exclaimed.

I stepped into the shop and he caught me in a hug which drew all eyes to us and brought tears to mine.

He set me at arm's length, still holding on to me. "Su, how didst thou get here? Did Will send for thee?"

"No. I came alone. Will doesn't know. I had to come; his letter, and thine, made me so afraid. Is he ill, Nat? Where is he? I went to your lodgings but the woman said to ask thee…"

"There's no need to fear."

He led me further into the shop and introduced me briefly to the other men as a Friend from home. The sound of the press, the smells of ink and paper, the printed sheets hanging to dry, were all familiar to me and, despite the noise and activity, somehow calming.

"He's with our Friend Edmund Ramsey," said Nat. "Edmund is a wealthy man, a merchant. He took Will from Newgate to care for him. Will has been very sick, but thou need not fear for him now. He is still living at Edmund Ramsey's house."

"And is he recovered?"

"I hear he is much improved."

So the two had not met recently.

"Where is this house? Is it near? I must see him."

"Throgmorton Street. It's near the Exchange. Not far." He glanced at his idle press. "I'll go there when I finish work – tell him thou'rt here." Then, seeing my face, he added, "Or I'll take thee."

"But, Nat, I can go myself, and see him at once." I couldn't bear to wait.

He ran an inky hand through his hair and frowned. "I wouldn't go there alone, Su. They're grand folk … big house…"

"I don't care about that! They're Friends, you say?

They won't refuse to let me in."

"No, of course not." But he still seemed uncertain. When he saw that I was determined to go alone he gave me directions and said, "I'll speak to thee tomorrow, perhaps, and hear thy news?"

"Yes, for sure. I'm staying at the Three Tuns in Martin's Lane."

So I left him. I could not wait, now, to find Will. I left Alum Court and, following Nat's instructions, found my way to Cheapside. Despite the press of people, there were still many shops closed and an atmosphere of dejection about the place as the light began to fade. The air was colder now, and I walked on quickly, looking about me till I came upon what must be the entrance to the Exchange. I stopped and gazed in at the large pillared courtyard, crowded with people, and surrounded on three sides by shops – two storeys of them – lit with candles that shone in the deepening dusk. I stood entranced, for I had seen nothing like it before.

A woman near by smiled at me. She wore a fine fur jacket cut low to show her white bosom.

"It's a sad sight," she said. "Half the shops still shut, and no one of quality here."

"But it's beautiful," I said.

She looked me over. "Down from the north, are you?"

"Yes." I began to retreat. I wanted to be on my way now.

But she laid a hand on my arm. "If you need a place to stay, I can help you."

I saw then what she was about, and said, "I thank thee, no," and moved quickly away. Instead I asked a respectable-looking maidservant, "Please, where is Throgmorton Street?"

She directed me, and was also able to describe Edmund Ramsey's house, so that as I came into the street I knew it at once.

Despite what I'd said to Nat, the sight of the great door did somewhat intimidate me. But I was no servant, and these were Friends; so I stepped up boldly and knocked.

A maid answered the door. She was simply but more finely dressed than I, and I half feared she might direct me to the back entrance. But she was pleasant spoken, and when I asked for Will she let me into the hall, which was panelled with a woven wall covering – green, with a damask pattern of birds and flowers.

From upstairs I heard music being played – and that surprised me.

The stairs were wide and polished to a deep shine. She led me up them, saying, over her shoulder, "He'll be in the drawing room, with the family."

We reached the landing. Now we were outside the room the music was coming from.

The door was open. She knocked, but was not heard: the music – a fast, merry tune – continued. I came to stand beside her and looked in and saw a grand bright room hung with damask fabric and lit by candles, and a group of people gathered around a keyboard instrument. There were several girls, one of them seated and playing; and Will stood among them, turning the pages for the player, who was a fair, pretty girl – the prettiest girl I had ever seen. She was playing fast. Her small white hands flew about the keys, and as she played she glanced up at Will, and the two of them laughed together. Will looked healthy, and well cared for, and the girls were like butterflies in their wide-skirted silk gowns: one gold, one green, and the musician in yellow as bright as her hair.

I stared at this scene – and suddenly one of the girls saw me, and said something, and they all looked up, startled. The music stopped.

Will gazed at me for an instant without recognition; and I knew he was seeing a country Friend come visiting in her heavy woollen skirts and black hat and sturdy shoes – one who meant nothing to him.

And then he knew me. A look of utter astonishment crossed his face. "Susanna!" he exclaimed – and he broke through the group and hastened towards me.

I turned and fled. I didn't want to be reunited with him in front of these girls. I'd had my answer. He was not ill. He did not need me. All I wanted now was to be gone, out of this house.

The maid had left. I ran down the stairs, reached the door, and grappled with the latch.

"Susanna! Don't go!" He was close behind me.

But the door was open. I was free. I plunged out into the street, and began running back the way I had come, towards the Exchange.

He followed me, shouting, "Su! Wait! It's dark…"

It *was* growing dark now, and that helped me escape. I darted behind a sedan chair carried by two serving men with link boys holding torches, and then around a group of maids laden with baskets. When I glanced back I could no longer see him.

I hurried on, head down, choking with tears. In my mind, I still saw him standing beside the yellow-haired girl, the two of them laughing together, the keys giving up their sparkling music under her hands. That's where he belongs, I thought; not with me. That's what he meant when he wrote: *my circumstances are quite changed*. And I knew I should never have come.

William

I ran after her as far as the Exchange, but she had gone. It was almost dark. Lamps had begun to appear above doorways all around, and the candlelit shops in the Exchange glimmered enticingly. Could she have run in there, I wondered? No. She'd have darted down some alley.

I stared about me, desperate. The streets were still busy; people were hurrying home from work and shops. I looked down several side streets and stopped passers-by and asked if they had seen a country girl in a high black hat, but Londoners walk fast and take no heed of others; no one had noticed her.

What to do now? I felt angry and helpless: furious with her for rushing out into the darkness of a strange city, and with myself for causing her distress.

I had no choice but to go back to the house. As I walked there – still in my indoor shoes, which were now soiled from the street – I saw the encounter as it must have appeared to her: the grand, intimidating house; myself, not ill as she'd perhaps imagined, but playing unseemly music and surrounded by fashionably dressed girls.

And yet Susanna wasn't one to be in awe of grand folk. I'd always thought she'd face anyone – the King himself – and not be daunted. Why had she run from me?

At the back of my mind, where I would have preferred to avoid it, lay the answer: Catherine Ramsey. I'd been looking at Catherine. The piece she was playing had been approaching its crescendo and she, delighting in her skill and control, had caught my eye and we had both laughed with the sheer joy of it. Nothing more. I knew there was nothing more. And if I'd ever had any doubts, the appearance of Susanna in the doorway had instantly dissolved them.

She'd be alone out there now in the darkening streets. I *had* to find her. Where had she come from? Some inn, I supposed. I thought about what I'd said in my last letter; then counted the days and realized it could not have reached Hemsbury before she left. So she hadn't read it – couldn't have known when she set out from Shropshire that I was with the Ramseys. Someone else had told her that. She must have spoken to Nat.

Back at the house, the door had been closed, and I had to knock to be readmitted. The maid, Sarah, looked at me with undisguised curiosity, but said nothing, except to enquire whether she should take my shoes for cleaning.

I gave her my shoes, asked her to tell the family I would not be home for supper, and raced upstairs in stockinged feet. The drawing-room door was, mercifully, shut, and there was no sign of any of the Ramsey girls – probably on their mother's orders. I'd have to face them – but not now. Now I must find Susanna. I flung on coat, hat, outdoor shoes, and left the house.

I'd go to Creed Lane. See Nat. He must know where she was.

Susanna

I hurried the length of Cheapside, but when I reached the dark bulk of Paul's I stopped and, for the first time, wondered where I was going. I could not remember the way to the Three Tuns, or to Creed Lane, or even Alum Court. Panic grew in me. People walked by so fast that I feared to stop them – and no one asked me if I needed help, as folk would at home on seeing a stranger who looked lost.

As I stood there, bewildered and afraid, a familiar figure emerged from a side street.

"Nat!" I cried. I flew into his arms and foolishly burst into a torrent of tears.

"Su! What's happened? Don't cry. Thou'rt safe now." He patted me, making soothing noises, while I gulped great sobs that kept rising up in my throat so that I could not speak.

He led me back to Creed Lane, to his lodgings, and asked if I wanted to come in, or would I rather sit with him in the Blue Boar, next door?

I knew it would be more seemly for us to go to the Blue Boar, but I could not bear the thought of folk looking at me, and said, in a small choked voice, "I'll come in."

Back home in Shropshire, I'd never have gone into a young man's lodgings with him, nor embraced him in the street; but London seemed to be a place of strangers where no one watched or cared. Nevertheless, the woman I'd spoken to earlier glanced at me, I thought, with mild interest as I followed Nat into his room.

It was a while before I stopped gulping and crying. Nat left me to it, and began trying to revive the fire, which had sunk to embers.

The room was cold. It was a low, cheerless, cramped space, the window overlooking a muddy yard. Out there I could see a midden and a privy, the smell of which drifted in, even though the window was closed. I sat on the only chair. There was a stool, and two beds – Nat's unmade, with a cat and kittens asleep in it, the other covered with a counterpane and several more kittens. A bowl of scummy water stood on the washstand.

The fire came to life, and smoke billowed briefly into the room. Nat poured me a mug of beer and picked up a kitten and gave it to me to hold.

I managed to laugh in spite of myself. "Is this thy cure for heartache?"

"Maybe."

I stroked the kitten and it kneaded my skirt with its tiny claws. A small purring came from it. Nat squatted beside me. "So what is this heartache? Didst thou find him? Thou weren't there long."

The tears spilled over again, and I brushed them away. "I made such a fool of myself. I shall never be able to meet those people again…" I raised my head and looked at him directly. "Nat, Will is in love with someone else."

"I don't think so."

He sounded so certain that my hopes were raised. But then he had not seen Will lately.

"There is a girl there," I said. "A daughter, I suppose?"

He nodded. "I believe there are several daughters."

"They were playing music on one of those keyboard instruments: a virginal, or harpsichord. He didn't see me at first." My throat was closing up; it was hard to talk. "They were looking into each other's eyes and laughing together."

Nat allowed the kitten to climb onto his knee. "It's not a crime to laugh," he said. "I do it myself, quite often."

"Don't mock me."

"I didn't mean to." The kitten moved between the two of us, purring. "I know he loves thee, Su. All this plague-time he has been desperate to go to thee."

"But thou knew *something*. Thou tried to warn me."

"Only because of the house. They are such fine folk, and live in grand style. It's a house that makes me feel out of place."

"But not Will. *He's* not out of place there. He belongs."

"Aye – he's settled in easily enough." He gave a little shrug and a rueful smile, and I wondered if he too felt rejected. He and Will had shared life and lodgings since they arrived in London together, but now, it seemed, a separation had come about.

"If it hadn't been for me," I said, "he'd have been living in a house like that these last three years. He'd expect to marry a girl like her."

"Su, he chose thee, and a different way—"

At that moment there was a knock on the door and Will's voice, raised and urgent, called out, "Nat? Art thou home?"

I sprang up. "I can't see him!"

But he was already in the room. His gaze alighted on me at once, and I saw relief flood his face. "Thank God!" he said.

"I must go." I had begun to tremble. "I'll be missed at the inn."

But he stood in my way, his face full of hurt and bewilderment. "Thou can't go! Talk to me, Susanna! It's been three years. I've worked and waited for thee. Thou can't refuse me even a word."

His voice had grown louder and I quailed before him.

Nat intervened. "Will, she's distressed. No good will come of this. You can talk tomorrow. Let her go now."

"And run out into the night again? Alone?"

"I'll walk with her."

They faced each other, and I felt caught between them. Will – hot, angry and thwarted – at last backed down.

He turned to me. "Will thou see me tomorrow?"

I nodded.

"Where is the inn?"

Nat replied, "Martin's Lane. The Three Tuns."

"I know it." He approached the door, then looked back at me, his eyes pleading. "Goodnight, Su."

Nat and I left soon after he had gone. I was subdued now, and felt an extraordinary tiredness sweeping over me. Nat delivered me safely to the inn door. Alice tactfully asked no questions, but I saw that she was concerned at my appearance. I went to the mirror and looked at my face. It was blotched pink, with swollen eyelids. Yet only a short time ago I'd been teasing out tendrils of hair, eager to appear at my best for Will. I thought about how he'd looked when he turned back to bid me goodnight. His was the face I'd carried in my heart and memory all this time, and had longed to see. I love him, I thought; but my mother was right: long ago she'd said to me, "He's not for thee, Susanna." I saw now that he had always been destined for someone like Edmund Ramsey's daughter.

My eyes were heavy. Alice ordered us a light supper in our room, but I scarcely touched the food. I went to bed early. All I wanted was to sleep.

It was as well I did sleep, for he came soon after six next morning. I was already dressed and sitting with Alice in silent prayer when a knock came on the chamber door and a serving girl told me there was a young man asking for me.

I followed the gleam of her candle as she led the way downstairs and into the main room of the inn. This too was lit with candles, for it was still dark outside. Several tables and benches were full with people eating breakfast. A fire of logs blazed and crackled in the hearth, and a party of newly arrived travellers stood around it, red-faced from the cold and blowing on their hands.

Will was sitting alone at a small table near a window, wrapped in a dark cloak and wearing a plain black hat. He rose at once to greet me.

"Susanna! It's early – I'm sorry – I could not wait…"

He reached instinctively towards me, and I knew that if we had not been in a public place all my resolve would have left me and I would have moved straight into his arms.

"Come. Sit down," he said.

The girl hovered. "Will you take breakfast, sir? We have an excellent pottage." She was looking at him with interest; he had those dark, lean looks that many girls like. And I thought of the Ramsey daughter.

We both declined the pottage, and asked for beer and bread. I sat down, determined not to be swayed from the decision I had made on waking. I looked directly at him and said, with difficulty, "Will, I release thee from thy promise to me. Thou need not feel bound by it."

He looked bewildered. "But I *wish* to feel bound! There are difficulties – I wrote to thee, but thou won't have had the letter…"

"Thou lov'st that girl – the musician."

"No!"

Other people looked round at us, and he continued in a low, intense voice, "Catherine is fond of music, as I am. I enjoy her company, but it's thee I love, Susanna."

Catherine. So that was her name. In my memory I saw them again: laughing, catching each other's eyes; saw their shared joy in the music. Perhaps he had not yet acknowledged it in his heart, but...

"Thou belong there, Will; can't thou see it? Those people, with their books and music, their wealth, their connections. I saw thee there, and my eyes were opened. I saw that I should never have come. Thou did not expect me, nor send for me—"

"Only because the time was not right!"

His voice had risen again. The girl arrived with the bread and beer, and her glance took in our quarrel as she set the food out on the table.

When she had gone, Will reached for my hand, but I withdrew it.

"Su, what you saw was nothing – nothing! I have never been alone with Catherine; I am not courting her; thou wrong'st her to think so. I have scarcely spoken to her of anything except music."

"But thou *lov'st* the music! I could see that. It shone in thy face. And with me, thou would lose it. I come of plain, sober folk. I have grown up without music. To me, it seems – not ungodly, but ... frivolous."

"It is frivolous indeed compared with my promise

to thee." And he looked at me with such hurt and longing that I was almost persuaded.

But I had made my decision. "I shall go back to Shropshire," I said, "and set thee free."

Our bread lay uneaten on the table. The newly arrived travellers settled near by and were served with bowls of steaming mutton pottage. They talked loudly, forcing Will to lean towards me as he tried to speak. I drew back, but he seized my hand and held it firmly.

"There is only one impediment to our marriage," he said, "and that is my lack of work and prospects. James Martell and all his family died of the plague."

I felt shock. I had not known this. "I am sorry, Will."

"Edmund Ramsey cared for me when I was ill and has given me employment, though it is temporary. That is the only reason I remain there. They are good people, Su, newly become Friends. I wish thou would meet them —"

"No!" The memory of my shaming flight from their house rose before me. "No, don't ask me to face them again. I shall go home. There is no place for me here."

William

I walked back to Throgmorton Street in despair that I had been unable to reach her, to make things right between us. What had happened to our love that we had nurtured through three years of letter-writing: talking of books, of religion, of places, Friends and friends, our ideas and dreams of life together?

Now that I had seen and spoken to her again I had no doubt that I wanted Susanna as my wife. For the first time, this morning, I'd had a chance to look at her and see how she had matured and changed since I'd seen her last. Her face, framed in the plain cap of unbleached linen, had lost some of its childish plumpness but none of its fair colour, so appealing in London where people mostly look pinched and pale. Her dark eyes and her voice with its soft country burr were as beautiful as I remembered them.

We loved each other. We belonged together. How could she think I'd prefer Catherine Ramsey?

It was true – more true than I'd admitted to Susanna – that I had felt drawn to Catherine, and not only because of our mutual love of music. She was there, in the house, a pretty girl who enjoyed and sought out my company. But she was also a virtuous girl, who had done nothing wrong. I reflected bitterly, self-pityingly, as I trudged back through the cold dawn streets, that I had stayed true to Susanna for three years, as I'd promised her; I had not had any other girl, nor gone whoring as many young men do. I did not deserve her censure. She wronged me; and wronged Catherine.

The Ramseys did not ask questions, but they knew something was amiss. That afternoon there was no virginal-playing, and I noticed that the music books had been put away.

Dorothy, the youngest girl, regarded me solemnly. "Thy Friend was shocked, I think."

"No, not shocked. But she – she felt unable to stay."

I guessed that Catherine – indeed, all the women in the household except Dorothy – had grasped the situation exactly.

"Is she thy sweetheart?" the child asked.

"Dorothy!" warned Jane.

Clearly they had been told not to talk about my visitor.

Catherine was quiet and avoided my eye. A constraint had come between us, and I suspected that she felt overcome with guilt, as I did. I feared also that she was disappointed – that she had more fondness for me than I'd realized, and was hurt. I knew I must be careful, now, to protect her honour.

I considered leaving Edmund's house at once and returning to Creed Lane. But that would imply that something had happened between me and Catherine, which it had not. So I stayed, and nobody mentioned Susanna, and over the next few days the atmosphere in the house returned to normal and I sometimes heard the virginal again in the afternoons. I spent most of my time in the library, hard at work. The cataloguing would soon be finished, and then I would leave.

On seventh-day, in the evening, I went to see Nat.

"Hast thou seen Susanna again?" I asked him.

"No." He looked at me warily. "You didn't kiss and make up, then?"

"No. We did not." I would not talk to him about our troubles, but added, "She said she'd go home."

"I doubt she'd go till the other Friends leave," said Nat. "Perhaps she'll be at the Bull and Mouth meeting tomorrow."

I thought about going to that meeting, where I could encounter her as if by chance. But what could we say to each other in company, even supposing she wished to speak to me?

She would not want me haunting her. I went with Edmund to Gracechurch Street instead.

Susanna

I did not go home. When I tried to imagine myself doing so I realized that I had nowhere to go – except back to Long Aston, and I didn't want that. I had ended my employment with Mary and had no place any more in her house. I thought, too, how humiliating it would be, to return to Hemsbury without Will; how I'd have to explain to Mary, to the Mintons, to Em; and be pitied by everyone.

So I told myself. No doubt there was a glimmer of hope there also, but I did not admit that.

I was certain I should not hold Will to his promise. He was with people of his own kind now, and I had seen how easily he consorted with them, and realized that he might soon begin to prosper again if he was not held back by me. I thought, too, how those people must have seen me – especially that fair, blue-eyed girl with her quicksilver hands. I'd stood there, dumbstruck, in my heavy shoes and plain hood and hat – a country girl whose hands were red and roughened from work. Of course the Ramsey girls were Friends, but as different from me as swans are from chickens.

I would give him his freedom, I decided. But I did not leave London.

The Shropshire Friends I had travelled with planned to leave in December – well before the shortest day and the feast of Christmas. That gave them some two or three weeks to visit London Friends and meetings. Some went to stay with relations or Friends they already knew; those few of us remaining were to be taken in by members of the local meetings.

On the first-day following our arrival, Alice and I went to the meeting at the Bull and Mouth tavern in Aldersgate. I knew this was the meeting Will and Nat usually attended. Nat was there, but not Will; and despite my resolution I felt disappointed. I was too proud to ask after him. He'd be with the Ramseys, I supposed, at some other meeting, or at their home; and the worm of jealousy, which I knew should have no place in my heart, twisted within me, and prevented me from reaching the light.

After the meeting, when we talked with Friends,

I was approached by a thin, pale young woman with sombre dark eyes. Her name was Rachel Chaney, and she offered me lodgings at her home.

"It would please me if thou would stay in my house while thou'rt in London," she said. "I am alone except for my young child. My husband is on a prison ship – condemned to be transported…"

"The *Black Spread-Eagle*?" I said.

"Thou hast heard of it?"

"Yes. And have been praying, in Hemsbury Meeting, for thy husband and the other prisoners." I understood now why she looked so wan. "I should be glad to stay with thee."

She smiled then, and the smile brightened and changed her face. "Come tonight," she said. "I live in Foster Lane, above the silversmith's workshop. It's near here. Thy friend Nat will show thee."

Nat came to the Three Tuns that evening and took me to Rachel's house. Alice had already gone to stay with a widow named Jane Catlin, who lived near by.

Foster Lane was only a short walk from the inn. It was a narrow lane, darkened by the jettied storeys that almost met overhead, so that on this winter evening we could see almost nothing except where an occasional household lantern cast a pool of light. I feared what I might be treading in, and stepped cautiously. The silversmith's shop was locked and shuttered, and entry to the house was by an even narrower passage between two shops which led to the back doors.

Rachel greeted us and invited us both in. Nat set down my bag while I looked around at the small kitchen, which was lit by tapers. There was a table criss-crossed with knife cuts, pewter plates on a rack, bunches of herbs hanging from the limewashed ceiling, and a baby's linen cloths drying on a guard by the fire. In one corner, safe behind a makeshift barrier, was the baby: a little girl less than two years old who reached up her arms to Nat and said, "Dadda!"

Nat shook his head and laughed, as did we all; and Rachel scooped up the child and kissed her and said, "She calls every man Dadda! I wish thou might see thy dadda soon, my poppet." She turned to me. "This is Tabitha. She was eleven months old when her father was sent to Newgate. I fear she will forget him, so I talk about him to her all the time. Nat, will thou take beer with us? I have bread and some cold mutton too."

But Nat said no; he'd leave us to talk. And he wished us goodnight and blew a kiss to Tabitha, which made her laugh; and then Rachel picked up a lighted taper and led me upstairs – she with the child on her hip, I with my bag.

There were two more rooms, both small, and one above the other, linked by steep, narrow stairs. Above the kitchen was a parlour, and above that a bedroom with a four-poster bed hung with thick drapes, a washstand, a child's cot, and a chest of a fashion I had not seen before, with drawers in it.

I set down my bag here, and went to the window to look out. There was no view, for the upper storey of the house opposite was almost close enough to touch. Someone with a candle was moving within.

Rachel said, "In summer, when the windows are open, we wave to Goody Prior, don't we, Tabby?"

We went downstairs to eat. I noticed that the fire was not lit in the parlour and guessed that Rachel was saving fuel by not using that room. It must be many months since she'd had her husband's income. In the tiny kitchen I amused Tabitha with a toy dog on wheels while Rachel mixed some gruel for the child, then cut up meat and bread and brought out a jar of pickled vegetables, and set the table.

"I'm glad thou could come," she said. "My mother wants me to go and stay with her, back home in Houndsditch; she says I should not be on my own. But I don't want to go back there. I got married in part to get away from home! Sit down, Susanna, and eat."

She took Tabitha on her lap and began spooning

gruel into the child's mouth. Tabitha struggled to seize the spoon herself, flicking gruel around, and then became more interested in what was on her mother's plate.

We tried to talk, but our conversation was broken by the child, who demanded attention. After supper she grew sleepy and her head lolled on Rachel's shoulder.

"I'll put her to bed," Rachel whispered, and crept upstairs with the little girl, whose face and hair were sticky with gruel.

She came down alone and said she would light the fire in the parlour, but I persuaded her not to. "It's warm here, by this fire."

"I try to save money," she said. "The meeting helps. Friends have been good to me."

I asked, tentatively, "What news of the *Black Spread-Eagle*?"

She paused, and looked down at her hands in her lap. "None, for some while. There was plague come on board, and many must have died, but we don't know who... The ship is still in the river—"

"*Still?*"

"Yes. It's been nearly four months now. They say it cannot sail because the master has been arrested for debt, or some such. Oh, he is a foul, worthless man! I know I should seek to see the light in everyone, but in him I cannot! He will be the death of my husband, who is a good Christian and seeks only to worship God in peace—"

Her voice broke, and I reached and touched her hand. "I'm sorry, I should not have..."

She looked at me, her eyes red. "No. I need to be angry. I am angry with Vincent too, for going to Meeting that day when he knew he was at risk." She brushed tears away. "He is a small man; slight, not strong – except in the spirit. His health is not good; every winter he suffers with a cough... But tell me about thyself, Susanna. Thou hast come with Friends to visit London meetings?"

"No," I confessed. "I may do that, but I came to find my – the man I promised to marry. Will Heywood."

"Oh!" She turned to me with renewed interest. "Thou'rt *that* Susanna! Will was to have been married to thee at midsummer?"

"Yes."

"Will is a fine young man. Serious and deep-thinking. Thou know he is at Edmund Ramsey's?"

"Yes." I didn't want to tell her, then, about my troubles; they seemed so trivial compared to hers. But she must have sensed that all was not well, for by the time we had washed the dishes and gone up to bed, she had teased it out of me.

"I think thou need have no fear," she said. She took off her cap and unpinned her hair, which fell dark and straight to below her shoulders. "He was eager to go, and to marry thee."

"But that was in the summer," I said. "He'd made no plans to come home since."

"But thou'll stay in London?"

I smiled. "*I* don't want to go home to my mother, either."

William

Susanna: thou may have released me from my promise, but I do not release thee—

No. That was too threatening. I tore up the paper and began again:

If thou would only hear what I have to say…

Too apologetic.

I should pursue her, I thought, insist on seeing her. But I feared another rejection. And what could I offer her when I had no work, no prospects, no proper home?

I put the pen and paper away. I would not approach her again, I decided, until I had found a new employer: a bookseller, or stationer, perhaps a notary or some such who needed a clerk; someone who'd give me full-time work that would pay enough to keep a modest household. There must be such work to be found.

Meanwhile, my time at Edmund Ramsey's was coming to an end. Within a week the cataloguing was finished and I arranged to leave. Working and living with the family, I had come to know them all well – the servants too. But my former ease with Catherine had never returned. I knew she was unhappy, and feared I was responsible for that. It was better to go. Edmund thanked me, said he'd recommend me to any prospective employer, that they'd miss me and I must come back and visit them – and then I returned to my old lodgings in Creed Lane.

It was a shock to be back in that unwholesome place, to have to find my own meals, do my own washing, and face empty days looking for employment. The room, which had been stifling in summer, was now, in December, cheerless and cold. I was glad to be reunited with Nat, but our old camaraderie had diminished with my long absence; and he was at work till the evenings.

The day after my return was my twenty-first birthday: my coming of age. I sat alone by the fire eating a bowl of day-old pease pudding while icy rain beat on the window. Had I been at home with my family I could have expected a celebration, perhaps a gift of money or clothes: certainly some recognition of the day.

I mused on what might have been, had I not fallen in with the Friends of Truth and left Hemsbury without my father's blessing. If I'd followed the road he'd laid out for me I would by now have been three years or more into my apprenticeship with Nicholas Barron. I'd have money, good lodgings, excellent prospects, and would have travelled in Europe. Nick Barron was an acquaintance and near neighbour of Edmund Ramsey, so I might well have met Catherine. I might have courted her and hoped, in due time, to be married, to the delight of both our families. And I'd have been free, after my apprenticeship, to join Friends if I wished.

But I had made my choice, and could not regret it. I had chosen independence, and Susanna. I thought, ironically, that now I was at last free to marry without my father's consent, I had neither the means nor the woman.

Susanna

$\mathcal{I}$ remained at Rachel's house while visiting London meetings with the other Shropshire Friends. We travelled to several meetings, but most of the time I was at home with Rachel, and we soon came to know each other well. I helped to mind the child, to cook, and to shop; and I made sure that I paid for my share of the food and fuel. In all that time – some two or three weeks – I did not see Will, though Nat (whom I met at the Bull and Mouth) told me Will had finished his cataloguing at Edmund Ramsey's and was back at Creed Lane and looking for other work.

"Does he enquire after me?"

I hadn't meant to ask, but couldn't help myself.

"He did once. And I told him thou were at Rachel's. Did I do right?"

I nodded, and bit my lip, not trusting myself to speak. I'd thought Will might try to see me again, but I'd heard nothing from him – no letter, not even a message. I should have been relieved, but I was not.

Sometimes, in bed at night, Rachel and I talked. It was easier then, when I could not see her face and knew she could not see mine, to talk about love: her love and mine, and what we should do, and what we might hope for. There was something that had been on my mind a long time, from before I left Hemsbury, that I wondered about whenever I imagined myself in bed with Will (which I did often, despite our rift). One night I asked her, "Rachel, dost think Will has ever had another girl?" I could feel myself blushing, and was glad of the darkness. "I don't mean Catherine Ramsey. Before that, dost think he ever…"

Rachel hesitated. "Thou mean…"

"Yes."

"I don't think so. No. Will is such an honest, upright young man, I can't imagine…"

"But it's been more than three years," I said.

"All the same, he'd have waited. People do."

As the time approached for the Shropshire Friends to return home, I talked to Nat about finding work. "Would thou ask Amos Bligh if he needs anyone?"

"Thou mean to stay in London, then?"

"Yes. I won't go home and be an old maid." I caught his eye and tried to laugh. "I'll be one here."

"And old maids – even young old maids – need employment?"

"Yes."

"I could ask him. We *are* a hand short: Jem Forrest went home to Hertford when the plague came; and Amos knows I plan to leave soon, and set up on my own."

"I couldn't replace *thee*!"

"No. But he might take thee on in place of Jem."

The next day I heard that Amos Bligh would see me, and went to the print shop in Alum Court. Nat's employer was a man of about forty years of age, born and bred in London, and trained as a printer from his youth. He had come to the truth some ten years ago and now printed many books, commentaries and court proceedings published by Friends; but, like Mary, he did not turn down any work unless he considered it unfitting.

He was wary of me, a woman so young and with no formal apprenticeship; but he questioned and tested me, and soon found I could deal with most aspects of the work except operating the press.

"Thou know'st typesetting too?" He seemed surprised.

"Yes. I have learned to do it. But mostly I worked on assembling pamphlets, and serving in the shop, and keeping accounts."

He looked relieved. "I could employ thee as a general assistant. If I took thee on as a typesetter there might be complaints as thou hast had no apprenticeship. But if thou could turn thy hand to whatever was needed..."

I knew this meant he'd pay me less than his printers; and a woman was paid less anyway; but I didn't mind. It was work, enough to live on and keep me in London. And while I was in London I was close to Will. I tried to put that thought out of my mind, but it was always there.

I made an offer to Rachel. "If I may stay with thee – if thou wish it – I'll pay thee a fair rent and my share of all expenses."

She agreed; and that night she lit the fire in the parlour, so we no longer had to dart through a chilly room and staircase to reach our bedchamber.

At work I soon felt at ease, as I had at Mary Faulkner's. The men were mostly Friends and all behaved discreetly towards me, from the boy, Joel, to old Thomas Lyle, the typesetter. I took home much more than I'd earned at Mary's, but these were London rates, and I reckoned Amos Bligh had his money's worth from me.

In the middle of December, Alice Betts and the other Shropshire Friends set off for home. Alice and I embraced, and she said she'd give news of me to Mary – "But not too much news, never fear! Only that thou'rt safe and well and with Friends."

"I thank thee, Alice."

I imagined their long cold journey, the fields and hillsides of my home country perhaps white already under snow, my parents and Deb stocked up with corn and salt pork for the winter, the trees dark and leafless now in the little wood where I'd hoped to walk with Will.

Here in London we had hard frosts, but no snow had yet fallen. Despite the grip of winter, the plague persisted. We still saw the searchers with their white staves in the streets, and sometimes the cross on a door. There was a charnel-house smell in Foster Lane that came from the overfilled burial ground of the steeple-house of Anne and Agnes near by. Rachel hung bunches of herbs around the house, and burned rosemary to clean the air.

Still I did not see Will. My spirits were low, despite my work and the friendship of Nat and Rachel. I saw now that I had deceived myself. I had given Will his freedom, but had not expected him to take it. I'd thought he would come after me; that I might resist him, but he'd still desire me; we'd quarrel, perhaps, but all would be resolved. Now I realized that he was avoiding me; and I felt resentful that for all his declaration of love it seemed he did not care enough to pursue me.

I would not go to him. I was too proud and too hurt.

The feast of Christmas came and went. People hung garlands on their doors and inside their houses; and in the markets there was greenery for sale, gathered and brought in by country folk. We Friends did not celebrate Christmas, though we were at Meeting on Christmas Eve, that being first-day. On Christmas Day the city streets were quiet except for the sound of church bells. Amos Bligh opened his shop as usual, and someone must have reported it, for he was arrested and taken to Wood Street counter, and later fined.

Nat had got into the habit of walking me home to Foster Lane in the dark evenings. It was only a step, but he insisted, and it became a companionable thing between us. Usually he left me at Rachel's door. Rachel was a young woman whose husband was away; the neighbours probably already regarded her with suspicion because she was a Quaker, so he was careful of her reputation. But one evening a sudden rainstorm sent us scurrying down the passage and we both fell into Rachel's kitchen, breathless, laughing and soaked. She hung up our cloaks and hats to dry and warmed some ale with spices in it, and insisted we all eat together before Nat went home.

Nat and I told her about our day at work, which had been busy, with a bothersome customer who was never satisfied; and Rachel laughed and said, "Thou'll be glad to leave, Nat!" and asked him about his plans to set up on his own.

"I'm minded to go to Bethnal Green, or Stepney," he said. "Rents are lower, and it's outside the reach of the guilds. Plenty of wealthy folk, scholars and such. I reckon a printer could do well there."

"A business of thy own," said Rachel. "What more could thou want?"

"A wife," said Nat. "And children. I'd like to marry."

And I thought: Yes, he's an orphan; never knew his parents. He'd want a family; it would be important to him.

Rachel was in a teasing mood. "Rebecca? Patience? Sarah?" She named girls at the Bull and Mouth meeting.

He shook his head and grinned. "None of them. I've no one in mind yet."

"Well, thou'd be quite a catch. Thy own master, hard-working, sober—"

"Free of the clap," added Nat.

I joined in the laughter despite myself; only Nat could get away with such talk without seeming offensive. Rachel exclaimed, "What would our sober Friends think? It's time thou left, Nat Lacon! Thy cloak is dry and the rain has stopped. Be on thy way!"

He went out, amid more banter.

Rachel was still smiling when she turned back to me. "Thou could do worse, Susanna."

"Nat?"

"He likes thee. And you're in the same trade. Suited. I'm sure half our friends already think—"

"I love Will," I said.

But now I wondered. I'd told Will – and believed it – that he belonged with people like the Ramseys; and if that was so, then surely I belonged with someone like Nat?

"He has a fondness for thee, I can tell," said Rachel.

"Oh! We've known each other for years. Worked together." I remembered how safe I'd felt when I ran into his arms that first evening in London, how he'd taken me home, and defended me from Will's anger. "We're like brother and sister."

A few days later I came home to find Rachel quite changed. I saw at once that something bad had happened, and a feeling of dread came over me.

"What is it? Thy husband…?"

"The *Black Spread-Eagle* has sailed."

"Oh, Rachel."

I put my arms around her. She was shaking.

"All this time," she said, "five months and more, I've kept a hope alive that they'd be released, that *someone* would declare the ship unfit to sail. So long as they were still in London it seemed possible…"

I could think of nothing to comfort her, except to say, "Whatever they must endure in Jamaica, it could not be worse than living below decks these last five months."

"I know. I hold to that. But – oh, I feel the loss of him now, so much more, knowing he is at sea and gone from me!"

We heard no more of the prison ship, except that it was probably on its way to Plymouth. Rachel was heavy with grief, and her misery affected me. But I too was unhappy. Weeks had passed since Christmas, and I had heard nothing from Will. I was in a strange city, in winter, far from home and family. I wondered why I remained here at all if Will did not want me, why everything had gone wrong, and what would become of me.

These thoughts were on my mind one evening as we were finishing work. Two printers were away with colds, and Amos had gone to deliver a late order himself. I was left sweeping up, alone except for Nat, who was tidying the fount cases while he waited to walk home with me.

I put away the broom, and went to fetch my cloak. Nat approached. "Ready to go?"

I looked up at him and nodded without speaking.

He must have seen my unhappiness in my face, for he stepped quickly towards me and put his arms around me and said, "Oh, Su!" I clung to him, burying my face in his shoulder, and he lowered his head so that our faces were touching. We stayed like that, unmoving, for several moments. I could smell the printer's ink on him, and feel the roughness of his chin against my cheek; and I knew for certain that if I turned my face even a little towards him my mouth would meet his, and we would kiss each other, and nothing would ever be the same between us again.

I was tempted, for I wanted love; and I saw now that it would, after all, be possible to love someone other than Will. But I did nothing; and it was Nat who moved, putting me gently away from him, and saying, "Let's get thee home."

William

I found a succession of jobs: swilling pots and unloading barrels at a waterfront tavern; running errands for a baker whose boy had died of the plague; packing orders, two days a week, for a hat-maker, a Friend, in King Street. There was plenty of work of a casual kind to be had as the plague retreated. By Christmas I had combined the daytime packing and the evening tavern work and was only at home three nights a week. It provided scarcely enough to live on, but left me free to search for something better.

Nat and I spent little time together. He was making plans to set up in business on his own and had a friend, a typesetter, whom he visited in Whitechapel some evenings. We would pass each other as we came in and out and, when we did meet, were often too tired to talk. I felt jealous of his good prospects and disappointed in my own efforts.

"It's not thy fault," he said. "There's a prejudice against incomers, especially Dissenters. When more businesses reopen thou'll find something."

He put a hand on my shoulder. "Let's go to the Crown tonight. It'll cheer thee. And it's warmer than this place."

So we went out, and ate and talked.

There had been much anxiety in the city of late about the new year that was coming: 1666. It was the date itself that was feared: the numbers 666, the mark of the Beast, the Devil. Our Friend Elizabeth Wright had seen visions of the city laid waste, Paul's steeple-house ruined and open to the stars. And there had been reports of strange-shaped clouds, a monstrous birth in Aldgate, a comet...

"But the comet was a year ago," said Nat. "And I reckon we've had our calamity already, with the plague."

"I've been reading," I said. "William Lilly, and others; Friends' writings..."

It seemed to me that there must be some pattern to these things, some meaning to be found, and I had been reading whatever books and pamphlets I could find and marking passages that particularly struck me.

Nat was not much of a reader and found such matters dark and not to his liking.

"But we've been printing plenty of such stuff," he said. "The shop's busy – uncommonly so. Lucky we took on Susanna."

Usually he was careful – we both were – not to mention Susanna, though I knew he must see her every day, and that he walked back with her to Rachel's each evening. He had told me, when the Shropshire Friends went home, that Susanna had not gone with them; but that was all.

"She is staying, then?" I said.

"Oh, yes. She will not leave now."

He spoke with certainty, and I thought: He knows her mind; she confides in him. I remembered a time in Hemsbury, years ago, when I'd glimpsed Nat and Susanna chatting, easy together – and I felt again a flicker of the jealousy I'd experienced that day. Then, it was easily dismissed; but now, Susanna and I were estranged.

Susanna

$\mathcal{I}$ looked at Nat differently now; I could not help it, even though nothing had happened; and I felt that he was aware of me in a new way. I noticed also that the men in the print shop seemed to regard us as a pair. Perhaps they always had, and I had been too caught up in my longing for Will to notice.

Nat treated me the same as ever. He tactfully avoided any mention of Will, but talked to me about work, mostly, or his plans to move out to east London.

"The towns there are thriving," he said. "Stepney has its own market. And there are gardens and orchards, some common land."

"I miss the countryside," I said. "Hemsbury was town enough for me."

He looked at me and smiled. "The sky was bigger in Shropshire."

"Yes. It was."

Was he wooing me, I wondered, with a promise of orchards and fields? He'd said he wanted a wife. He was twenty-five, and would be settled enough, soon, to marry. And I'd be able to help him run his printing business; I knew the work well enough.

I *could* love him, I thought; if he wants me, I believe I could.

We were finishing work one afternoon when Nat told me, "I'm going out east tonight. There's a place in Bethnal Green I want to see: a shop and workroom, with living quarters above."

It was seventh-day, early in February. We'd had to light candles to work by, the day was so dark, and the fire seemed to give out no heat. We all wore hats and heavy woollen jackets, and as Nat and I talked our breath clouded the air.

"They say it'll snow tonight," I said.

Joel had already reported seeing a few flakes when he went out to the yard.

"Oh, I won't come back till tomorrow," said Nat. "I'll lie at Laurence Elvin's, in Whitechapel. I want to see this place; it'll mean waiting till next week, else."

I could see he was excited and hopeful.

We left and walked back together to Foster Lane. Nat was quiet. At first I assumed he was thinking about the premises in Bethnal Green; but several times he glanced at me and seemed as if he might say something, then changed his mind.

He is about to speak of love – of marriage, I thought.

My heart began to race, and by the time we arrived at Rachel's door I was as uncertain and nervous as he. What would he say? What would *I* say?

"Susanna" – he reached inside his cloak and pulled out a letter – "this came for thee this morning."

"This?" I was confused, my expectations overturned.

"Yes. By rights I should have given it to Will, but he'd already left for work, and – well, it's addressed to thee…"

I took the letter. It had been sealed and posted, that much I could see, but in the dark street I couldn't make out the writing.

"What — ?" I began.

But Nat said, "Take it. I'm off to the Elvins'." He paused, then stooped and kissed me briefly on the lips. "Read thy letter. I'll see thee on second-day."

And he turned down the alley, out of sight.

I hurried inside, and joined Rachel by the fire, where she was stirring stew in a pot. I felt bewildered, taken by surprise. And the letter… When I looked at the writing on it I began to tremble with anticipation. It was from Will, addressed to me at Mary Faulkner's shop; but that address had been crossed out, and Mary had replaced it with Will's address in Creed Lane. Rachel watched as I opened it.

"It must have arrived in Hemsbury after I left," I said, "and been all this time on the road…"

My hands were shaking as I unfolded the letter. It was dated the fifteenth of November: a week before I arrived in London and saw Will at Edmund Ramsey's house.

Dearest love,

I should have written to thee more fully before, but I am only now sufficiently removed from all that has happened to be able to speak of these things…

Rachel touched my arm. "I've lit the fire in the parlour. Go and read it in private."

"I will."

I took a candle, hurried upstairs, and pulled a stool close to the fire. There were several pages, densely written, and as I read them I began at last to have a sense of all that had befallen Will since the summer.

He spoke briefly of his suffering in prison, for he was not seeking sympathy but offering explanation.

From the hints he gave I saw that he had endured cruel, bestial treatment, meted out over many weeks, and the thought of it filled me with anger and horror and made me weep. He blamed himself for the deaths of his two friends, and had been still weak from his own illness when he heard of the deaths of the Martell family, and with them the loss of all his hopes of partnership in the business and marriage to me. Edmund Ramsey had rescued him, probably saved his life, and cared for him at his own expense, so it was no wonder that he had been happy in that house – so clean and kind and comforting – which reminded him of his parents' home.

He said nothing of Catherine Ramsey, except that she and her sisters were *pleasant girls, and good-natured, but with little knowledge of the world and the hardships many Friends experience.* If he has any affection for Catherine, I realized, it is no more than I have felt for Nat – and probably less. He should have equal cause for jealousy. But I knew now that I need have no doubt of him; his love for me shone through every word.

I saw that I had been wrong. I had acted on nothing but my own hurt feelings and had never thought of his. He had made no plans to travel to Hemsbury because he was unable to offer me a home and an income, and felt he could no longer expect me to marry him.

And yet, there is nothing I desire more.

I folded the letter and put it in a pocket under my skirt. I must go to him, I decided. And I would not wait till morning. We had both waited long enough.

I ran downstairs and found my cloak and hat.

"I have to see Will," I said to Rachel. I hesitated, thinking of the likely consequences of my action. "Don't stay up for me."

She was rocking the sleepy child on her lap. She did not seem surprised, or shocked; merely asked, "Won't thou eat first?"

"I'm not hungry."

"Well, it'll keep."

I opened the door and stepped out into the cold night. Snow was beginning to fall. I had never been out alone in London so late before, but I was not afraid; I had too much on my mind. My desire to reach Will gave me speed, and I hurried down Foster Lane, then along Paternoster Row, around the great dark mass of Paul's steeple-house. Few people were about: a nightwatchman, beggars huddled in doorways. By the time I reached Creed Lane the snow was falling faster and the cobbles glistened where pools of lamplight caught them. I ran till I came to Thomas Corder's house.

I never stopped to ask myself if Will would want me, whether I might have offended and hurt him too much. I saw a light within, and knocked at the outer door. A man opened it; I asked for Will, and he looked me over, no doubt wondering what sort of woman I was. He let me in and knocked on Will's door, calling, "Mr Heywood!"

And then Will was standing there, startled, his hair rumpled, an old coat thrown around his shoulders. He stared at me, and I saw his look change from astonishment to joy.

"I had to come—" I began.

His arms went round me, and he pulled me into the room and shut the door and held me close against his heart.

"Su!" he said. "Su…" And then: "Thy hands are cold! Thou'rt wet from the snow. Come and get warm. This fire's not much."

He seized a poker and jabbed at the sulky coals, causing a brief crackle of flame; sparks flew up the chimney. A small black and white cat on the hearthrug coiled itself into a tighter knot.

"It's a cold, miserable room, this," Will said, as I began taking off my hat and hood. "I often get into bed to keep warm—"

He broke off and reddened. Both of us glanced at the beds.

"Nat will stay in Whitechapel tonight," he said.

"I know. He told me."

I saw him absorb the significance of this remark. Would he think me brazen? I had surprised myself, coming here when I knew he'd be alone. I trembled as I said, "Thy letter came," and brought it out of my pocket.

He was puzzled. "Letter?" And then, seeing it: "Thou read *this*? I thought it lost…"

"Seems it was, until today. Nat brought it to me."

"If it had come while I was here, I'd probably have thrown it on the fire. I'd almost given up hope of thee, Su."

I put my arms around him, told him how wrong I'd been, how sorry I was.

"I should have come after thee," he said. "I was too proud."

There was only one chair in the room, so we sat on the bed, and then lay upon it, and forgave each other with kisses and caresses. His body hardened against mine and I trembled with feelings so strong they took me by surprise. We had been separated for more than three years, but any strangeness that had come between us in that time melted away. We've been mad, I thought, to stay apart these last long weeks. I wanted never to let go of him again.

But even as we kissed I felt him holding back

somewhat, and at last, to my disappointment, he pulled away. We sat up, both of us hot and flushed, and he took hold of my hands and looked at me with that serious look I remembered and loved, and said, "Su, we should not… I have no proper employment now, only what work I can find here and there; not sufficient to marry on. And no home to take thee to. Thy parents would not be willing—"

"Oh! They would!" I said. "They *are*. I have their permission to marry."

"But that was last summer, when my prospects were good."

"Thou'll find something else."

"It's not easy, without training, and with few skills."

"But thou hast *some* work. And I do, too."

"That's different!" he said. And I saw that I had hurt his pride.

"I trust thee to care for me," I said. "And as for my parents, they married without money or permission. My mother ran away from home." I laughed. "They lived 'like the birds of the air', she says, and trusted in God, who has held them in his love ever since."

"The birds of the air." He smiled, and pulled me closer, till our noses bumped together.

"Or the lilies of the field," I said. "Though we did toil much, and my mother spins for a living."

"I should like to know thy mother better. Thy father too."

"So thou shall, if thou marry me."

"Did they name thee for the lilies of the field? Susanna: it means 'lily'."

"Does it? They found it in the Bible; I doubt they knew its meaning. I did not."

He'd lost me again, with his books and learning. But I felt pleased to be a lily.

The serious look in his eyes had been replaced with expectancy. "Then thou hast no fears? We'll marry, shall we? Here in London? Without prospects? Without a home?"

"I want a *home*!" I said. "Thou needn't think I'd live here, not even with thee."

He laughed. "We'll find somewhere. There are plenty of places – and all must be better than this." His eyes brightened at the prospect. Then he said, "Su, I'm hungry. I bought a pie in Pudding Lane on my way home. Shall we share it?"

The pie was a poor thing, but it staved off hunger. After we had eaten, we sat on his bed, close together, and drank warm ale, and kissed, and talked. What we talked about, I don't remember, but I know that all the time I was thinking, as he must have been, of what might come next.

Gradually we talked less, and kissed more, and the

feel and smell of him made me want to gather him in to me, as if we could never be close enough; and I knew he felt the same.

We heard faintly, from a neighbouring street, the nightwatchman's call: "Nine o'clock, and all's well!"

I broke free then. I went to the window and stood with my back to Will, looking out at the yard and passageway. Snow lay thick on the ground, and big soft flakes fell steadily against the window and built up on the ledge, cocooning us.

"If I'm to get home…" I began.

He came and stood behind me, put his hands on my arms, kissed the nape of my neck.

"Don't go," he said. "Stay with me, Susanna. Please."

I woke in the night when some revellers went by outside, shouting. For an instant I did not know where I was, and then I remembered, and felt his arm under my shoulders, the heat of his body against mine, his steady breathing. From the edge of the bed came an icy draught, and I pulled the blankets close and snuggled against him and felt his other arm reach around me as he slept.

Our coming together had not been quite as I'd imagined it. First there were the cumbersome layers of winter clothes. I insisted that the candles be blown out before I began to undress. The room was cold, and I was nervous and kept my shift on as I got under the covers. It was a shock to feel him climb in beside me and to realize that he was naked. I was tense, and I knew he was anxious; the passion of only a few minutes ago had cooled: we tussled awkwardly and nothing seemed to be right. After a while he rolled away and we both apologized.

"It doesn't matter," I said.

But I felt that it did; that I was to blame.

I sat up and took off my shift, then slid back and put my arms around him, laying my body alongside his.

That must have been what was needed, for all at once we were together again, both of us moving without thought or fear, as if we'd always known what to do. And although in the end it was clumsy, uncomfortable and too quick, I didn't mind. I lay beneath him, feeling the thudding of his heart, with a sense of both contentment and triumph.

We belong to each other now, I thought. We shall never be parted again, except by death.

I'd known all along what would happen if I entered his room that night. But since we had renewed our promises to marry, there seemed no wrong in it; indeed, it seemed a right and honest thing to do. I had said to him once, of Friends: "We try to live in the truth"; and our love *was* the truth.

I woke again, a little before dawn. Something was treading on the bed: I could feel feet – an animal! I opened my eyes and saw the small black cat with white whiskers peering at me over the edge of the coverlet.

Will half woke, muttered, "Go away, cat!" and shook it off. He reached for me, and we rolled together, warm and expectant. The cat returned, pressing and purring, and I started to laugh.

Will said, "I'll put it out."

He got up, caught the cat, and darted naked to the door. I heard a muffled exclamation, and almost at once he was back beside me. "Ma Corder was outside!"

"Oh, Will!"

We shook with laughter; and then began to kiss and stroke each other. This time, when he moved to lie on top of me, everything seemed easier; and though I hurt a little afterwards I felt truly happy.

Next time I woke it was full day. There was a cold, clear light in the room, and a strident sound: the bell of Paul's steeple-house.

"Will," I said.

He opened his eyes – grey-green, flecked with gold – and smiled at me; and at once I wanted to stay there with him, wrapped in his arms, all morning. But I said, "It's first-day."

I had quite forgotten, until I heard the bell.

He came properly awake. "Then we must go to Meeting."

"Together?"

Despite my determination to be truthful, it might appear unseemly, I thought, to walk boldly in like man and wife.

"Rachel will know already," said Will.

We dressed quickly, both shy now, turning away from each other, and laughing as we shivered and drew on layer after layer: in my case shift, stays, bodice, jacket and two woollen skirts. I combed my hair, looking in Will's mirror, and marvelled that I did not look any different to yesterday although I felt such momentous change in myself.

We breakfasted on stale bread and beer, and let in the cat, which was mewing and scrabbling at the door.

"We'll have no cats in our home," said Will.

"Then we'll have mice."

"And thou'll leap on a chair."

"I will not!"

We continued with such foolish talk while we ate, and then we became serious and sat in silence awhile, to prepare ourselves for Meeting.

Corder's wife was at her door to make me blush as we emerged together into the sound of bells from all over the city. The overnight snow had hardened to a bright frost which crunched underfoot as we walked to Aldersgate.

We went first to Rachel's house. She was just leaving, with Tabitha toddling alongside. I blushed again on encountering Rachel, and did not know what to say, but she merely remarked, with a smile, "We shall have a wedding, then, soon?"

And I thought: Yes, we shall. Will and I would not, after all, wait till spring to go home and be married at Eaton Bellamy Meeting with my parents and Isaac and Deb there to wish us well. We would be married here, in London, where our new life was about to begin.

William

That morning, when I woke and found Susanna beside me, I experienced a wondrous, drowsy mix of happiness, pride and contentment. I wanted to stay in bed and prolong our time there, for I knew we would not be together again until we were married. But I also felt a certain guilt, and a desire to protect her, and I knew that I must set about finding somewhere for us to live.

I began my search the next day.

The city was full of vacant houses and rooms, many at very low rents, but there was good reason for this. The first place I saw looked a handsome house, and the whole upper storey was vacant, but at a suspiciously low rent.

"You won't find better value," the agent assured me.

"Is it a plague house?"

He shrugged. "The plague was everywhere, last summer."

"But people died here?"

"It has been aired and fumigated. Thoroughly smoked throughout, the hangings changed…"

I did not even go in. Something in his manner made me distrustful. I knew I should not give in to fear. I should put my trust in God. But I had Susanna to care for now, and was fearful on her behalf. Coming fresh from the country, she might be more likely to fall victim to the plague. And the sickness was still about, though the death toll was falling. Fourth-day that week was another day of fasting and prayer in the churches, and Friends closed their businesses and went to meeting.

We heard that the King, who had been in Oxford, had returned to London, and this made us feel confident that the greatest danger from plague must be over. But there was no more news yet of the *Black Spread-Eagle*.

At the end of the week, Susanna and I went together after work to see a place in Bow Lane, which runs south from Cheapside. The house was next to the steeple-house called Mary Aldermary, built close up against it, so that on the north side it was shaded by the tower. The ground floor was a hosier's, with living quarters and storage above, and an attic floor to let: two rooms, furnished, at a reasonable rent.

We climbed the narrow back stairs and found ourselves in a low attic room. The window was small and the ceiling sloped towards it.

"Oh! I like this view!" said Susanna.

I stooped, and looked out over a spread of rooftops, jetties, innumerable chimneys with smoke rising up and, far below, glimpses of people thronging the darkening streets. I saw a few lanterns already glowing, the moving lights of link boys, and the flicker of candles in windows. So many people live in this city, I thought; so many other lives. I could not see the river, but saw a slender crescent moon, which pleased me after the view of the privy at Creed Lane.

The walls were limewashed and the floor made of clean boards, and there was a table and stools, and a small fireplace with a pot and trivet for cooking.

The hosier's wife stood at the top of the stairs, watching us. "It is all newly done," she said. "And quite high, in the centre."

I removed my hat as it knocked against the ceiling.

A doorway led to a second room that contained a bed, washstand and clothes chest. It too had a low window, but the light was stopped by the nearness of the steeple-house. The walls were painted reddish-brown. As we stood looking around, a great sound of bells burst from the steeple-house next door, seeming to rock the walls of the room. We both gasped and clutched each other in shock, then began to shake with laughter.

"Bell-ringing practice," the hosier's wife said. "Every Friday night. You get used to it."

"We wouldn't lie in on first-days here!" I murmured to Susanna, who was still trying to stifle her laughter.

We came back into the parlour, where Susanna examined the cooking area and looked at me in approval.

"It's a long way to carry water," I warned her, "up all those stairs."

She shrugged. "Oh, I'm strong!"

"Thou like it here, then?"

"I do. I like to be high above the city. And thee?"

I agreed. There was a madness about the place that appealed to me: an eyrie, blasted by bells, where I would knock my head at every turn; and yet I could imagine us making a home here.

"Let's take it," she said. And we exchanged a smile, secret and complicit. Now we could be wed.

As we followed the woman downstairs I took Susanna's hand and felt her fingers curl in to mine.

"Quakers, aren't you?" the woman said. I realized

that mixed, perhaps, with her fear of Dissenters was a feeling that Quakers were unlikely to use the furniture for firewood or make off without paying the rent. I gave her a crown piece as deposit and agreed to move in next week. She produced an account book in which she asked me to write my name or make my mark; I signed it, and she wrote down the five shillings and made her own mark – a cross – beside my name.

Susanna and I were married at the Bull and Mouth meeting nine days later, on Susanna's nineteenth birthday. The meeting was full of our friends, for everyone likes a wedding, and there were many young children present. Edmund Ramsey came with all his family, dressed in subdued fashion and sitting unobtrusively near the back – which I liked him for, being concerned that the Ramsey presence might disconcert Susanna.

But I soon saw that nothing could unsettle Susanna today. Her face, framed by the plain linen cap, was calm, her hands loose in her lap. I felt all around us the support and well-wishing of the meeting, and knew she must feel it too. The silence grew, broken only by some fidgeting and babble of small children. I meditated on marriage, my responsibilities as a husband, wondered what our future would hold, and thought about how we might serve God more fully together than separately. At first I slid a few glances at her, but she had closed her eyes, and after a while I ceased to think about my surroundings and withdrew into the inward light, and felt the meeting become gathered.

The silence was long and deep, as befitted our serious undertaking. At last the atmosphere changed; I heard a rustle of movement, and Jane Catlin rose to her feet and said that we had all come here today to bear witness to the marriage of William and Susanna.

"We are not here to join these two in marriage as the priests do," she said. "We are but witnesses. The marriage is the work of the Lord."

Then I caught Susanna's eye, and together we rose to our feet and took each other by both hands.

I said, "I, William Heywood, take thee, my Friend Susanna Thorn, to be my wife. And I promise that with God's help I will be to thee a loving and faithful husband until death shall separate us."

I spoke with much intensity, and felt tears spring to my eyes and saw an answering glitter in hers. But she spoke out light and clear, in much the same words, ending, as I had, "until death shall separate us".

Until death shall separate us. There was death all around us in the city, and danger at every turn, from sickness, accident or persecution. Only God knew how long we would have together. We must live every moment of our time fully and in the light.

After we had spoken, there was another brief silence, and then the meeting broke up with smiles and good wishes. Rachel Chaney came and put her arms around me and wished us happiness, and as I returned her embrace and felt how small and thin she was, I became aware more than ever of the fragility of life and the need to use it well.

"God keep thy husband in the light, Rachel," I said, "and bring him safe home to thee."

Nat embraced us both, and so did Jane Catlin, and Hannah Palmer, and others – including Edmund Ramsey, who spoke warmly to us both and introduced Susanna to his wife and daughters. If Susanna felt any awkwardness with them, she did not show it.

Afterwards we had a wedding breakfast with Friends at the inn, and then Susanna and I left together and walked to our new home.

"Oh!" said Susanna. "Someone has been here!"

The fire was lit, there was a white linen cloth on the table, bread, milk, and a bowl of fruit; and bunches of dried lavender lay on the bed and window sills.

Susanna smiled. "Rachel, I reckon. And Hannah. They left the inn early."

I put my arms around her, held her close.

"Sometimes I thought this day would never come."

"I feared that too."

"Thou don't mind that it was not at Eaton Bellamy? Will thy mother mind?"

"No. I think she expected it. She gave me my wedding gift: this shift."

"Shift?"

She looked at me and sighed, mock despairing. "Thou hast not even noticed! It is new. My parents made it for me."

I looked at the shift where it showed in the neckline of her dress and below the hem of her sleeves. "It's very fine," I said – though for the life of me I could not see it to be much different to any other shift. "But I shall like thee better without it."

"Thou promised thou'd take me to see London Bridge this afternoon."

"I did. And I shall."

It was a fine, cold day, the sun bringing some winter brightness. The filth of the streets had hardened under the ice and walking was cleaner than of late, though slippery. We held hands.

"Londoners are dirty," Susanna said. "And the people are rude. They don't give you good morning."

"If they said good morning to everyone they met it would take all day."

"But they push past and are always in a hurry."

"Thou'll get used to it." I felt a moment's anxiety. "Thou won't want to go home?"

She held my hand tightly. "No! I belong here now, with thee. I shall learn to love it."

So we walked to the bridge, and Susanna marvelled at the tall houses, several storeys high, built all along its length, narrowing and shading the roadway below; at the carved woodwork and gilding, the grand shopfronts, the domes and weathervanes of Nonsuch House. Her excitement inspired me, and I pointed out the sweep of the river, full of little craft upstream; and downstream, beyond the Tower, the tall masts of seagoing ships. We walked to the Southwark side, passing under a score of skulls impaled on poles and picked clean by birds.

Susanna glanced up. "Traitors?"

"Yes. Some of those who signed Charles the First's death warrant are there."

I led her ashore. "Shall we take a boat to Whitehall?"

We did, and saw the King's palace and the park they call St James's – a great space of trees and water – and from there walked east to Charing Cross. We stopped at a street vendor's and bought spiced warm ale and pies, then made our way home along Fleet Street as dusk was falling, and through Ludgate into the city.

The day had grown much colder, and Susanna shivered. We went around the north side of Paul's because I did not like passing James Martell's shuttered shop, and so to Bow Lane and up the narrow stairs to our home.

"Oh, it's cold!" Susanna held her hands to the fire.

"Come to bed, then."

It still felt strange to undress in front of each other, but with the shutters closed it was almost dark in the room. I was quicker than her, and turned to see her laying aside her stays. She stood barefoot in her shift, her hair falling in loose curls over her shoulders. I took her in my arms, my hands under her shift. "Take this off. Spare thy mother's needlework."

She laughed, and complied, but sprang quickly into bed and under the covers. As I got in beside her the bell of Mary Aldermary began to sound for evening prayers.

Susanna

I wrote to all my family and friends to tell of our marriage: my parents; my brother, Isaac; Mary Faulkner; and other Friends in Hemsbury. I bought paper and ink and a new quill from Amos Bligh and took pleasure in spreading my good news.

Will was reading. He watched me, somewhat wistfully, I thought. He had no one to write to.

I folded another letter, then melted wax in the candle flame and dropped it onto the letter and sealed it. "Won't thou write to thy father?" I asked.

At once his face took on a closed expression.

"There is no reason to," he said. "He has disowned me."

I knew, because he had told me during our three-year correspondence, that he had long since given up writing to his father; he had sent letters for the first few months, but his father had kept his word and had not replied, and his silence had hardened Will's heart.

I got up and went to Will, and kneeled beside his chair.

"Thou might end that silence with this news," I said.

"Hardly. Thou know'st what he called thee – how he insulted thee and told me that a girl like thee could never be daughter to him. I've broken with him, Su. I chose thee."

"But it hurts thee," I said. "I know it does. And it hurts him too. I told thee he came to see me in Hemsbury?"

"Yes – and was churlish to thee, by the sound of it."

"I can forgive him that."

"I can't. He has cast me off, and wants nothing more of me. He'll care not whether I've married thee or no."

His body felt stiff. I knew he was wrong not to try to heal the rift. "Write to thy sister, then?"

"Anne can scarcely read."

"Send her a token – a drawing, with our names. She'll understand. She always took thy part."

He smiled, and I felt the tension leave him a little.

"Maybe," he said. "But I don't want to involve her in secrets. If she fears to tell…"

"Why should she fear? We are wed now; it is done. And thou'rt of age and free to marry without consent."

"Yes." He hugged me close. "That's all that matters. Hast thou sealed thy letter to Mary? Let me add a few words."

It was a time for letters. One morning came the longed-for letter from Judith, sent on to me from Hemsbury by Mary, and telling of the Kite family's safe arrival in the New World – I calculated on my fingers that little Benjamin was now nearly a year old. Judith was not much practised at writing, and her letter was short, but her happiness and excitement were clear enough. Dan had found work as a blacksmith and they had a temporary home on the outskirts of Boston. *There are some here that do not love the truth, but many will listen,* she wrote. She spoke more of a mother's concerns: the long voyage; Benjamin's teething and how someone had given her a smooth peg for him to bite on and brewed a tisane for his fever; the friends they had made on arrival. *We are happy to be here, and grateful for God's goodness.*

I shared the letter with Will. Now we had an address and could tell Judith and Dan of our marriage.

The other news that came threw us all into alarm. We heard that the *Black Spread-Eagle* had at last sailed from Plymouth on the twenty-seventh of February, only to be captured the next day by a Dutch privateer and taken to the port of Hoorn in Holland.

Rachel, when we went to see her, was both relieved that Vincent was not yet transported to Jamaica and yet in dread that the Dutch, our enemies, would keep him prisoner. It was the first time the war with Holland had touched us directly.

"The Dutch will not want to keep them," Will said. "They'll try and exchange them as prisoners of war."

"But England will never agree to that! Not for Dissenters! They'll abandon them; leave them in a Dutch jail." Rachel's face showed the strain of months of waiting.

"If they do, Friends will work to get them released," Will assured her.

We sat in silence together and waited on God. I knew Rachel must have been thinking, as I was, that there might be few prisoners left to release; and I closed my eyes and sought the light that is in all people, of whatever religion, and prayed for a good outcome.

It was not long before we heard more news. I had returned from work one afternoon, and was alone, preparing supper, when I heard rapid footsteps followed by a loud knocking at our door. I opened it to Rachel.

"Su!" She was distraught, white-faced. "The prisoners are back! The Dutch have no use for them – they've sent them home. They are at Newgate – those who have survived…"

"Thy husband…?"

"I don't know. I must go there, Su. Will thou come with me? I'm so afraid…"

"For sure," I said – though I dreaded it. "Where's Tabitha?"

"At home. Sarah Chandler's there."

I left the food, and a note for Will, and went out with her at once.

She explained, "Sarah came to me. She'd been to visit her cousin in Newgate and heard that the Dutch prisoners, as they called them, were back."

Her teeth were chattering. I took her hand as we walked, and prayed that she would find Vincent alive and that I would be strong enough to help her through this ordeal.

I had never been inside Newgate jail before. Will had told me what it was like, but nothing he said could have prepared me for the stench and squalor and ungodliness of that place. The guards – one bloated and indifferent, another eyeing us both up in a lewd manner – mocked Rachel as she asked for information.

"Vincent Chaney," she said. "He is with the Quaker prisoners from Holland."

The fat one spat. "Quakers! Do you think we know the name of every Quaker in this place?"

"He was on the *Black Spread-Eagle*. Friends told me those prisoners are here."

"They came yesterday," I insisted.

The other man said that he'd heard "a lot of praying and preaching going on down there", and demanded money if we were to see them.

Rachel had known she would have to pay. She gave what they asked, and the second man led us down passageways so thick with dirt and ordure that even the walls were encrusted. The smell made my stomach heave, and I pressed my hands to my mouth, to the guard's amusement.

Behind closed doors we heard screams, curses, raving, and a general drunken racket. Will had told me that most of those who could afford to do so drank themselves insensible.

Our people were in a separate cell. The guard unlocked it, flung open the door, and held up his lantern. I heard a rattle of chains as the inmates turned towards us.

"See one you fancy?" the guard asked Rachel.

There were a dozen or more men in the cell: all of them thin, bearded, with long matted hair and staring eyes, all with running sores on their faces and bodies. Their clothes were dark with grease and sweat, and several were unable to stand upright, but moved as if they were still below decks.

I had never met Vincent Chaney, nor any of these men. I waited, in scarcely bearable suspense, as Rachel stepped in among them, her gaze darting from one to another, her hands held up, ready to reach out to him. "Vincent? Husband…?"

One of the men – wild-looking, filthy, his arms blackened with bruises – spoke in a voice of extreme gentleness. "He is not here, Rachel."

She sagged at the knees, and I ran forward and caught and held her. "Oh, Rachel! I'm sorry…" I turned to the man, who I now saw was quite young, not the bowed old man I had at first thought. "He is dead?"

"Yes." He looked pityingly at Rachel, who said, "Thomas? I did not know thee at first… Tell me – when did my husband die? How?" And her fingers dug into my shoulder.

"Last summer," said Thomas. "He was not with us long. Only a week after we went on board he was struck down with a fever and bloody flux. We had no physician. We cared for him as best we could, and prayed with him. He died knowing the love of God, Rachel."

She was silent; even her breathing seemed stilled. "I thank thee," she said at last.

Another man, whose lips were scabbed and peeling, spoke haltingly, with a thickened tongue. "He talked much of thee and little Tabby at the end."

Rachel's lips trembled. She looked around the cell. "Friends, I pray God you will soon all be released."

Throughout this encounter the turnkey had stood leaning against the door, picking his nails. He spat into the straw as we turned to leave, my arm supporting Rachel.

"All this time," she said, as we walked back into daylight, "I feared plague, and then shipwreck, or slavery. All this time his body has been lying in a common burial pit, or thrown overboard." She gave a little gulping sound, half sob, half laugh. "I don't even know which."

"He is not in any such place now," I said. "He is with God, beyond all hurt."

I did not know how to comfort her, but she clung to me as if my mere presence was enough.

Later that day, Jane Catlin, Sarah Chandler and I sat with her as she gave way to grief, and wept. Her mother, a formidable woman who had no time for Quakers, came and took charge of Tabitha and told Rachel that she and the child should come back to the family home in Houndsditch. Rachel resisted, but suffered her mother to take Tabitha there for a few days. She told me, "I must sell Vincent's stock and tools, now I know he is gone. I hope Tabby and I can stay on here if the workshop is let. I've no trade, Su. Not like thee. Unless it be to take in sewing, or some such."

"Friends will help," I said. But I felt how hard it must be for a widow; not only the lack of money and support, but to be without a man's love and companionship. We'd talked often of such love when I lodged with her, and I knew she missed it, and was lonely. Now I thought of Will, and how happy we were, and how joyously we greeted each other when we came home each day, and I truly believed I would die if I lost him.

William

Of the fifty-five prisoners on the *Black Spread-Eagle* only twenty-eight had returned alive to London. News gradually came to us in our meetings of their suffering during the seven months aboard the ship. The women had fared better than the men since they had been allowed on deck, but the men had been confined below the whole time, and more than half of them had died.

Susanna spent time with Rachel, often going to her house in the afternoons, after work. I was on my way to meet her there one seventh-day evening when I passed James Martell's shop and saw that it was unlocked, the door standing open, and voices and movement inside.

I stopped. I'd known, of course, that James Martell's relations must have inherited the stock, but I had grown used to seeing the shop locked and shuttered. All the books, as well as the Martells' personal possessions, were within.

A man – middle-aged and of prosperous appearance – came out. My concern made me bold, and I stepped up to him and asked, "Is the shop to reopen?"

He glanced at me without interest; I suppose I looked young and poor.

"Possibly," he said. "I am here merely to remove the contents."

I saw a likeness in his face to James Martell. This must be the brother he'd told me of. They had not been close.

"I used to work here," I said.

He looked at me more keenly then. "You're a Quaker?"

"Yes."

"The place is half full of Quaker books and pamphlets. Would your people buy them? Take the lot?"

"I would think so – if they can."

"There are booksellers around who might buy most of the stock; but the Quaker stuff…" He waved a hand in a gesture of dismissal. "Whom do I call on?" he asked. "Who's in charge?"

"I'll speak to the meeting," I said, "tomorrow."

He hesitated. I could see he thought me too young

to deal with. I said, "We have elders. I know the meeting will want these books."

"Very well." He told me he was Richard Martell, a mercer, and that we would find his shop at Aldgate.

I spoke to Friends after Meeting next day. There was a general feeling that we should try not only to buy such books as we could afford, but to keep the shop in Friends' hands, if someone could be found to rent it. The word would be put about.

A few days later, Edmund Ramsey came to see me at home. He arrived, somewhat breathless, at the top of our stairs, admired our little parlour and the view from the window, then accepted a mug of beer from Susanna and put a proposal to me.

It seemed that the Leighton brothers had told him about the shop and he had been inspired to take it on. He had made an offer to Richard Martell to buy all the stock and to the landlord to rent the premises.

"Now: I have my own business, as thou know," he said, "and no time or inclination to run a shop, although I have an interest in books. What if I employ thee as manager? No one seems better suited. Thou worked for James Martell for three years and must know the business well."

"I do," I said. I had a sense of a great burden being lifted, of a new opportunity. "I would willingly take it on."

He must have seen from my face how happy I was at the prospect. To be manager of a shop, and one that I knew and cared about, was the best offer I could have wished for. Now I no longer needed to feel that I had married too hastily. Susanna and I could live well enough on my wages. I glanced at her and saw that she agreed.

"Thou might wish to take on an assistant," Edmund said, "though for a while, at least, it may be that Susanna—"

"Yes," she said. "I know the work, and Will and I could run the shop together. I'd like nothing better."

He smiled. "Then we have a bargain. It seems the landlord does not offer the living quarters with the shop. He finds it more profitable to let them separately, and is asking a high rent."

"No matter," said Susanna. "We have a home, and are happy here." She was sitting close by me, and took my hand, unseen. Our fingers twined. I knew she would not have wanted to move; she loved our attic, as I did. Everything had come right for us at last.

We knew the shop had already been aired and fumigated, but Edmund feared that books and papers left dusty could harbour the pestilence, and before we took over he employed some women to take everything off the shelves and dust and wash all the surfaces and smoke the place again. On the day Susanna and I took up our new employment, a pale spring sunlight lit the rooms and showed us empty shelves and books piled high around them on the floor.

I walked among the stacks of shelves and remembered my good employer and his wife, and the small earnest face of six-year-old Agnes as she sat on the floor, a book open on her lap, reading to her brother.

Edmund must have guessed how I was feeling.

"We will keep the name – James Martell – on the shopfront," he said. "It is his only memorial."

The room smelled clean, herb-scented and smoky. But still we had not done, for Edmund had brought gunpowder to drive out any lingering breath of the plague. Some people fire guns in the room, but Edmund favoured sprinkling a trace of the black powder in a dish and setting off a small charge in two or three places around the shop. The flash was alarming, but afterwards the air seemed brighter and fresher, and I believe it was beneficial.

After this final cleansing came the task of replacing all the books, arranging the stationery, setting up the counter and a box for money, and preparing a new account book, ready for the shop to be reopened in two days' time.

At last we were done – all three of us dusty, tired and thirsty. We locked up, and walked to the nearby Bell Inn for supper.

Before we began to eat we sat a moment in silence. Then Edmund said, "Friends, it is God's work we do. This venture of ours will be a source of truth and light in the city."

Susanna

The summer of 1666 was the happiest of my life so far. It was hot – from May onwards the hot, dry weather continued, much like the summer before, and folk feared a return of the plague, which had never quite died out. But Will and I had no fears. In our new-found happiness we felt immortal. We had our home, our work, and our love for each other. I gave up my employment with Amos Bligh and joined Will some days in the bookshop, where we soon found James Martell's old customers began to return, pleased to find the place open again. I was glad of my training with Mary Faulkner and knew I was an asset, both to my husband and to his employer. We sold all manner of books, as well as Friends' writings, and Will sought out hard-to-find copies and ordered stock from as far afield as Oxford and Antwerp.

On the days when I was not working with Will I shopped in the markets: the Stocks or Newgate for meat, Aldersgate for herbs and roots. Sometimes I strayed into Cheapside or the Exchange to look at the jewellery, fine gloves, silks, and suchlike vanity displayed there. These goods, for all their worldliness, I could not resist seeing and admiring, even though I did not desire such things. I did, however, buy myself a gown – some wealthier woman's cast-off – from the stall of a trader recommended to me by our landlord's wife.

"You may be sure her stock is clean and not much worn – and she never buys plague goods," she said.

The gown I chose was a soft green, the neck rather low – but I covered that with a collar, and took the waist in to fit me. Will was much pleased with it.

Our attic home I kept clean and simple. We bought wooden plates and tankards, and a cooking pot or two, and I hung herbs from the ceiling where it was highest. I cooked on the trivet – "proper food", I told Will, for the London way of running to the shops for everything shocked me; and I made bread and took it to a baker's to be cooked. For our bedroom I hemmed sheets, and hung curtains around the bed, and stored our small stock of linen between layers of lavender in the chest.

That attic bedroom became for us the centre of our

world – so much so that I sometimes feared we were in spiritual peril, and ought to think more of our souls. But if I had ever dreamed of having Will in my arms in the meadow at Long Aston, now I longed each evening for our time together in that little room within sight and sound of the steeple-house of Mary Aldermary. The room was north-facing, and for that we were grateful, and for the shelter of the tower, which kept it dark and cool as the heat of summer advanced.

I came to love Mary Aldermary, for all it was a steeple-house. Its close presence and booming bells spoke of home to me; and its tower was a landmark as I moved about the city. Though I never went inside, I was happy to live in its shadow and to have landlords who worshipped there and were part of the life of its parish. At the north end of the lane was the great steeple-house of Mary le Bow, and all up and down were shops, inns and ordinaries where we might eat. From the southern end I could see down towards the river, though the wharf of Queenhithe was hidden behind houses.

Nat came to see us often, and sometimes all three of us would go out east to Mile End Green, where Friends' meetings were held. Nat's interest in premises at Bethnal Green had fallen through, but now he looked set to rent another place – a workshop with rooms above in Stepney – when it became vacant in August. He was full of plans and enthusiasm and talked much with us about it.

I was glad nothing had happened between Nat and me to put a constraint on our friendship now. He seemed the same as always, but for a while I wondered how he felt, if he was disappointed, even if I'd imagined his intentions. I'd never know for sure.

I also visited Rachel, who slowly emerged from her well of grief, helped by the need to care for Tabitha.

She had begun to take in sewing – plain work that as a Friend she could approve, and that she could do with the child playing near by.

"I used to work as a maidservant," she said – and I could tell from her voice that she missed it. "In a silversmith's shop in Cheapside. That's where I met Vincent. He'd bring in his finished work to be sold there. My mother never liked him; said he'd come to no good end, with his 'quaking'." She managed a trembling smile.

"He died bravely, in the truth," I said, "as we all hope to do if we must." But I wondered if I should be so brave when my time came, or whether I could bear it if Will put his life in danger again, even for the truth.

As spring turned into summer I had something more immediate to wonder about. The sun blazed down every day, and the filth and smells of the city would have been unbearable had Will and I not been high above them all, in our eyrie, as he called it. But the heat rose through the building and made our rooms a furnace; and though we threw open the windows not a breath of wind came through. One night towards the end of June we heard, from our bedroom, the reverse peeling of bells a little way off, and cries of "Fire!" This was so common a sound that I did no more than get up and glance out, and, seeing the smoke some streets away, took no more notice.

"The city is a tinderbox," said Will. "So tight packed with wooden buildings."

But the fire was far off, to the north-west. And I had something else on my mind.

"Will … hast thou noticed? I have missed my terms these last two months…"

He had been lying stretched out, lazy, trying to get cool.

Now he sat up, and I had all his attention.

"Thou'rt with child?"

I saw the gleam of his eyes in the darkness but not their expression.

"Art thou pleased?"

For answer he hugged me close and covered my face with kisses. "How could I not be? Clever girl! Clever me! We lack nothing now."

"Perhaps a cradle?"

"Thou shall have a cradle. We'll have one made. Carved with flowers and hearts—"

"No such vanity! It must be plain."

He laughed. "I was thinking of our family cradle at home: it's old, passed down; it has borders of leaves and berries, dark and shiny with age. Someone took joy in its making. That will go to Anne one day, no doubt."

"We should tell thy father this news," I said. "It will be his grandchild."

"Maybe… When we are sure."

"I am sure now. Quite sure."

But I knew he would not write. He had never written, even to Anne, about our marriage.

I wrote to my own parents, and had back a letter from my father telling of their joy and their longing to see me: *but do not think to travel – the heat is too great, and there is plague in the country. Thy mother urges thee to think much on God's grace, to eat fresh meat only, and new eggs, and to avoid parsley…*

Mary Faulkner responded with similar advice, and Rachel rejoiced in my happiness and looked out some little garments that had been Tabitha's.

Tabitha was growing fast. She was rosy fair and blue-eyed – like her father, Rachel said. He will live on in her, I thought. And I wondered what *my* child would be like, whether it would be boy or girl, whether brown eyes or grey – or even blue, like my mother's. Would it have Heywood looks? The Heywoods should be told our news, I thought again.

Will and Nat had begun occasionally visiting more distant meetings, in Middlesex, Essex and Surrey. Often I went with them, for I liked to go into the countryside. Once we took a boat across the river and walked through Redriff and Deptford and out to a meeting at Greenwich. We bought strawberries from a farmer's stall, and ate them with the bread and cheese we'd brought; and I picked wayside flowers: daisies and cornflowers. I thought of my coming child, how I'd like to bring it up in a place like this, with fields and trees and healthier air.

I felt no fear that my child would die, though so many do, at birth or soon after. Nor did the thought of the birth frighten me yet; I was strong, and believed I would bear a healthy child safely. But I knew Will was afraid for me, for my life. He became overprotective towards me, and I had to remind him I was a country girl, well used to lifting and carrying. I carried on working as before, and had no sickness. I looked no different either, except that I needed to loosen my bodice a little. But in my heart I felt different, and I knew I must give out happiness as the sun gives out heat. Only one thing concerned me as the weeks went by: that Will had not told his father our news.

One day, when he was at work in the bookshop, I came to a decision. I would write to Henry Heywood myself. He was my kinsman now, after all; and if he did not know that, then all the more reason to tell him. If the pair of them – Will and his father – were too proud to break their silence I must do it for them.

It was a difficult letter to write. Twice I changed my mind and tore what I'd written into pieces, wasting precious paper. I stopped, put down my pen, and sat in silence, and waited on the inward light. Then I grew more certain, and knew I must reach out to the light in Henry Heywood. I took up my pen again, and this time I wrote fast and simply, from the heart. I told him that Will and I loved each other and had stayed true for four years; that on the eighteenth of February we had been married according to the custom of the Friends of Truth – and before witnesses, I added, so that there could be no dispute.

Now, by God's grace, I am carrying thy son's child, thy grandchild. It is my wish that this child may heal the breach between thee and Will, which I know hurts him, and will hurt more when he has a child of his own. I do not ask that thou accept me, or forgive me, or even that thou forgive Will, only that thou may show

thy love to him (for I know thou must love him) and be
the first to write...

I sealed the letter quickly, before I could change my mind. After it was given to the post, I thought I should tell Will what I had done. But now my courage failed me. He might be angry, and I could not bear that. And his father might not – probably would not – reply; and then it might be better for Will not to have known anything. So the days slipped by, and I said nothing. And no letter came from Henry Heywood.

The summer continued hot and dry, but the plague declined, at least in London, and the traders and gentry had now all returned to the city. Those Friends still surviving in Newgate were gradually released; it seemed the authorities had other concerns now than to persecute us, and for that we were thankful.

Nat took over the premises in Stepney, and began setting up his print shop, buying an old press and getting the cases made for the letters. He put word about that he'd be needing an apprentice.

At the beginning of September, Will said he and Nat planned to go on first-day to a meeting in Kent where a travelling Friend was to speak: one well known for his visionary preaching. It was a long walk. They'd go with several others from our meeting and would not be back till late. He asked if I would come, but it sounded tiring, the weather being so hot. Much as I liked to be in the countryside I said I'd go instead to the Bull and Mouth meeting with Rachel.

In the early hours of first-day morning, the second of September, the wind grew to gale force; our shutters rattled, and the sign over the hosier's shop below squeaked as it swung; the whole house seemed to creak and groan as the wind found its way through every crack. We slept fitfully, woken by the wind and the heat in the room, and were up before dawn.

I packed Will a dinner of bread and bacon, an early apple from the market, and a leather flask of beer. I went downstairs with him, and we stepped outside together. Beyond the Tower the dawn sky was obscured by a haze of smoke from early-morning hearth fires. The day was as yet cool, and the gale still blew from the east, making me shiver.

Will wrapped his arms around me. "There's smoke on the wind."

"Always is."

But now we heard in the distance the reverse peeling of bells, and drums beating, and shouts and cries.

"Another fire," said Will.

We withdrew into the shelter of the doorway and embraced.

"Take care, love," I said. I hated being separated from him, and half wished, now, that I'd agreed to go too. "Will thou be back by sunset?"

"Sooner than that. And I'll bring thee some country flowers."

We kissed goodbye, and he set off uphill; he paused to wave on the corner of Watling Street, and then was gone from view.

I wrinkled my nose against the smoke and went back indoors.

William

I met Nat in Creed Lane, and from there the two of us walked to Paul's Wharf. A clamour of firefighting came from the east, and we saw a cloud of smoke streaming towards us on the wind. More boats than usual were out, some crowded with people, but these had come from the fire area; Paul's Wharf was quiet. We found a boatman, and embarked. As we pulled away from the shore into the centre of the river I saw with shock that the northern end of the bridge was in flames.

"The bridge!"

We stared, horrified, at the gap where a row of tall houses had stood. With the pall of smoke rushing towards us, it was difficult to see what else might be aflame.

Our boatman was full of news.

"Fire broke out in Pudding Lane, in the small hours. It's hot as Hell over there: melted lead from St Margaret's roof running down Fish Street Hill. Huge explosion in Pudding Lane; blew the street open. If you ask me, it's the French or the Dutch behind it…"

Nat and I exchanged a sceptical glance. There were always rumours of invasion, but the war was not something that much affected us: it took place mainly in the North Sea, and we read about its progress in the *Gazette*.

"Flames'll fly along the docks in this wind," the boatman said, almost with relish – and I felt a moment's unease.

But we had reached Southwark, and from here the fire looked less. It was too common a sight to worry us for long. We met with others at a Southwark Friends' house, and a group of us set off south for Beckenham, where one Ebenezer Trembath, a Friend from Cornwall, was visiting and might speak if the spirit moved him. He was, by all accounts, not a quiet seeker after the light but a fiery character, much given to prophecy, and I was eager to hear him and to take note of what he said for circulation around our meetings.

On the way, Nat and I talked about plans for his business. He'd written to Mary Faulkner, who encouraged him in the venture. He wanted to print and sell Friends' writings – perhaps eventually to have a bookshop, like hers. But that was all in the future.

"I'm stretching myself," he said – and he grinned and walked with arms spread wide. "The equipment has cost so much there's little left to employ others, except an apprentice. I'll have to work all hours."

"But it'll pay for itself in time," I said, "once thou become known."

"Yes. And *thou* might write some more. Think how pleased Mary would be to receive a pamphlet written by William Heywood and published by Nathaniel Lacon, Printer, of Stepney in Middlesex."

We laughed, but it could happen. I'd begun writing while I worked for James Martell: commentaries, reports and reflections. It had been strange and exciting to see one of them printed by Amos Bligh, and my name on it, and to know it would be circulated among distant Friends. What would my father make of it, I wondered, if it found its way to Mary's bookshop in Hemsbury? Would he be proud – or would he be enraged and think I'd brought his good name into disrepute? Well, he'd be unlikely to see it; and I had no connection with him now, except his name.

We walked on. The day should have been fair

for walking, but the gale from the east made it uncomfortable. We were glad at last to reach our destination: a village not far from Beckenham. Nearly a hundred people were gathered there. The plan had been to meet outside, but the wind drove us indoors, where we remained for several hours.

What can I say of that meeting? It was deep, certainly, and silent for a long time; later, several were moved to speak, and Ebenezer Trembath held us with his visions. But all this was overshadowed, cast into the recesses of memory, by what happened afterwards.

The village was isolated, and it was first-day, when few people travel, so we had no warning until we were on our homeward journey. At Herne Hill a countrywoman who let us draw water from her well said she'd heard there was a great fire burning in London – and, indeed, we saw a dark cloud to the north that must mean the fire had spread.

"It was prophesied," the woman said, and spoke of the comet and a blazing star, and a neighbour who'd seen a cloud shaped like an angel with a flaming sword pointing towards London. "It's God's punishment for the evil ways of the city."

I felt a touch of fear, a presentiment. Ebenezer Trembath's utterances had unnerved me and heightened my imagination. He had called London "the great Babylon" and quoted from Revelation: "'Babylon the great is fallen, is fallen, and is become the habitation of devils, and the hold of every foul spirit, and a cage of every unclean and hateful bird… Therefore shall her plagues come in one day, death, and mourning, and famine; and she shall be utterly burned with fire.'"

It might be true, I reflected, that the King and his court were deep in sin, but also in that great Babylon were many good people, and innocent, among them my love, Susanna, and our unborn child. I longed for wings to reach her. But we were on foot, and could make our way only slowly. All my thoughts were now on home. I would not stop to rest or eat, and I forgot to pick the flowers I'd promised Susanna.

As we approached Southwark we saw clearly, in the distance, a great mass of smoke, reddened underneath with flame, but could not tell how far it had spread. It was not until we came, at last, within sight of the river that we realized an area west of the Tower was all ablaze, smoke streaming on the wind, and a line of flame along the docks. Now we heard the sound of the fire: a deep, thunderous roar, and felt its heat, even from across the river. Smouldering fragments showered down upon us. I saw that the flames had spread west along the waterfront almost as far as the Vintry. Only a few streets north of there was my home.

"Nat! We have to get a boat!" I turned to the wharves where boatloads of shocked and clamorous people were struggling ashore with their possessions.

Our Southwark Friends began to look to how they might help those coming off the boats and find shelter for them. We left them to their work and made our way through the crowds to the waterside.

It was easy enough to find a place in a boat going the other way. All the boats and lighters were out, crossing and recrossing the river – the cost of the passage no doubt rising each time. We were overcharged on the grounds of danger. Nat wanted to argue, but I brought out enough money for both of us and thrust it at the man. I was desperate and would not delay further.

We asked for Three Cranes Stairs, but the boatman said we'd never get through the throng there. "The King and the Duke of York are at Three Cranes. They've ordered houses to be pulled down to make a firebreak. I'll take you to Paul's."

As we drew closer to the northern side, fire drops fell like rain upon us, stinging our faces and smouldering on our clothes so that we had to beat them out. Smoke filled my throat. The roar of the fire was now the background to a hungry crackling, as if some great beast were devouring the wooden buildings. We heard explosions and saw gouts of flame leap up where none had been before.

At Paul's Wharf a crowd was waiting to embark. We sprang ashore and began to squeeze our way through the crush of people. Only now, as I saw the streets blocked with carts, horses and panic-stricken citizens, did I realize how long it might take me to reach Susanna.

Nat came with me, for it was clear that the Corders' house in Creed Lane was not in danger, and we thought best to stay together. There was anger in the crowd, a need to blame someone, and it could easily turn against Dissenters.

A frightened man ran past us, his breath coming in great gasps. He was pursued by others, shouting.

"That Frenchman! I saw him put something through the window and then the house went up in flames!"

They surged along the street. What would become of the Frenchman if they caught him, I wondered? *Could* there be French or Dutch agents in the city firing buildings at random? Could it be the prelude to an invasion? And even if they were agents of an earthly power, was God using them to destroy the great Babylon?

"Will! We must go up towards Paul's – out of this smoke!" Nat steered me into a side street and we hurried, heads down, towards the steeple-house. All the time the main movement of people was towards the river, but the narrow streets caused panic. A fight broke out as two carts became jammed ahead of us. We turned aside and ran down a lane, trying to keep a sense of direction, for the familiar city was changed by the smoke and chaos.

We emerged east of Paul's, and found our way blocked by a detachment of the trained bands, armed with swords and muskets.

Their captain – young, with pale blue eyes, the whites smoke-reddened, in a soot-streaked face – demanded to know who we were, where we were going. They were looking for fire-raisers, anyone suspicious, and I hoped we didn't stand out as Dissenters.

"Where have you come from?"

"Southwark. We're trying to get home."

"What work do you do? Where do you live?"

"Printer," Nat gasped, coughing. "Alum Court."

They searched him roughly, finding nothing.

Then one of them seized me and pulled out the notes I'd taken at the meeting that morning. He showed them to the captain, who demanded of me, "What's this?"

He couldn't read, I realized with relief.

"Notes from a customer," I said. "I'm a bookseller. Here, in Paul's Churchyard."

He frowned, stared at the paper, then at me. He'd been told to intercept suspicious-looking men, and I saw that he had half a mind to take us into custody. I began to panic.

"Please!" I begged. "My wife is at home in Bow Lane. She's with child. I must reach her." And, when he hesitated: "I am a bookseller – no enemy to the King. Please. My wife…"

"On your way."

Relief flooded me as he thrust the paper back at me and let us pass.

"They need men at the fire-front!" he called, as we hurried away. "See you give help."

Bow Lane was free of fire, though smoke blew across the entire city, and from the top of the lane we could hear the noise of firefighting and see black smoke and flames bursting from a warehouse near Three Cranes.

Our landlord, Robert Whitman, was not in, nor his wife, and I saw that their cart had gone from the yard at the back.

I ran upstairs; shouted Susanna's name.

She was there. We caught each other on the stairs and clung together, oblivious to the presence of Nat, who must have retreated discreetly around the bend of the staircase. He reappeared when he heard us talking.

"The Whitmans are at Holborn," she said. "At his cousin's house. They've been back and forth with the cart all afternoon, taking their stock there for storage. They'll be back later."

"They left thee alone?" I said, and pictured her gazing out across the river, wondering when I would return.

"Friends came from the Bull and Mouth: Gerard Palmer and Jane Catlin. They are using it as a gathering point for Friends. We may store our goods there, and sleep there tonight if the fire drives us from home."

"Did thou go to Meeting?"

"Yes. Morning and afternoon. Jane said I should stay there, for safety, but I wanted to wait for thee. Oh, I'm so relieved to see thee, Will! And thee too, Nat." She reached out to him. "Come in, both of you. I'll fetch beer and food. You must be hungry."

"Thou should have stayed with Friends," I chided her, but I was glad she had not, that she was here, that our home was safe.

We drank beer, and I felt it cooling my scorched throat.

"Was Rachel at the Bull and Mouth?" Nat asked.

"Yes. She went home afterwards. Joseph Leighton walked with her."

Nat wiped his mouth with his hand. "I'll go to the meeting room. Call in on Rachel on the way and make sure she lacks nothing."

"It's quieter up there, near Aldersgate," Susanna said. "Much like normal."

But we knew that if the fire wasn't curbed soon, supplies of food and other necessities would run short, with the streets so clogged with people and shopkeepers deserting their premises.

When Nat had gone, Susanna put her arms around me. "I thank God thou'rt home. We don't need to leave, do we?"

"Not yet." I looked over her head at our meagre furnishings. "But they say the cost of a cart is rising by the hour. If the fire comes any closer…"

Her embrace tightened. "I don't want to leave our home."

We heard a voice on the stairs: our landlady, Ancret Whitman. "Mistress Heywood! Are you there?"

We both came out onto the landing. She stood a few steps below us, smuts on her face, her hands dirty and her hair escaping its cap.

"Oh! You are home, Mr Heywood! I'm glad. We were concerned for your wife." Her eyes widened.

"We have just seen the King! Such a handsome man! Working and encouraging others. The Duke of York too. They're down at Three Cranes. If you hurry you might see them."

We did not go. But towards sunset I walked down towards Thames Street and helped for a while filling and passing buckets with the firefighters. The street had been dug up and the water pipe breached, but the water supply was running low. Desperate people, whose homes lay near by, cursed papists and foreigners indiscriminately.

"They burned the waterwheel!"

"It's gone?"

"This morning, early. Utterly destroyed."

And there was more talk of the fire being a plot, the work of foreign agents. "The tide out, the waterwheel struck, then the bridge and docks…"

After a few hours I went home, exhausted by the long day. I spoke to the Whitmans, who had decided to stay in their home, at least till morning. I said we'd do the same. Susanna and I prayed together, and I read aloud from the Bible: not the terrors of Revelation, but the Twenty-third Psalm, which Susanna loved because its green pastures and still waters made her think of home.

That night we woke frequently, disturbed by the distant roar of fire and the shouts of men. Towards morning they seemed louder.

So London still burns, I thought.

We rolled together and held each other close, both of us unwilling to get up and face the day.

Susanna

We dressed in reddish darkness. I don't know what o'clock it was, or whether the sun ever rose that day. The clouds of smoke were lit by vivid flame, and when we went outside we found ourselves choking, gasping for breath, the air thick with smoke-borne fragments.

Down towards Queenhithe the smoke was blacker still, and as I stared with stinging eyes, I heard an explosion and saw a sudden uprush of fire – as high as a house. It was followed by screaming and the appearance of frightened people struggling up the lane towards us with horses, carts, children, bundles of belongings. The roar and crackle of the fire, the screaming and shouting and rumble of carts, brought me to a state of panic.

"Will! We must go!"

Our landlords were already loading up their cart – this time with their home possessions.

"Bring your things down," Ancret Whitman said to us. "We'll find room for them. You'll never get a cart for hire now."

"But where are you going?" Will asked.

"We have family in Holborn. We'll go there. And you?"

"The Bull and Mouth tavern," said Will. And he told Robert Whitman how to find it.

"We'll take you there, then leave by Newgate. It'll be better to turn north, I reckon, than try Ludgate."

We thanked them. We had little enough to save, but we took down our bed curtains and bundled up our sheets and clothes and kitchen things, our books and papers. I saw the home we had made together stripped bare, only the bunches of herbs left hanging from the ceiling as we turned to leave.

"Oh, Will!" I said. I felt heartbroken.

He hugged me to him. "We may yet come back. Let's hope."

He lifted the bedding roll, and I followed him downstairs with another bundle, and the Whitmans found space for everything.

We made slow progress up Bow Lane, which was blocked by laden carts. The smoke seared my lungs, and I found a strip of linen and tore it into four pieces, so that we could each hold a piece over our mouths.

Ancret Whitman was concerned for me, knowing I was with child. "You could ride in the cart," she said. But I refused. I feared the jolting would be worse than our shuffling walk.

At last we came out into Cheapside and even more confusion. In Jewellers' Row men were removing the precious stock and loading it into secure carts. All the other shopkeepers were employed in the same task, with carts waiting outside almost every door, and a great press of people, each intent on saving his own goods. People fleeing from Eastcheap said they'd seen the flames leap across streets, jump from one building to another five or six doors away. The docks were alight as far as Baynard's Castle, and the wind had veered north-east and was spreading the fire into Cannon Street. Our attic was surely doomed.

As we moved slowly north-east the smoke grew less and we were able to breathe more freely. We'll be safe at the Bull and Mouth, I thought. The fire won't reach there. The tavern was far away from the fire, near Foster Lane and Aldersgate.

The Whitmans took us almost to the door, and waited while we checked that there was room within. We thanked them for their kindness.

"We'll meet again soon, I hope," Ancret said,

"if God spares our house – and the church." Her husband was a churchwarden at Mary Aldermary, and much involved with parish matters.

I thought of Mary Aldermary, that place I'd given the slighting name of "steeple-house", and realized that I too would feel something precious had been lost if it was to burn.

The Whitmans drove off towards Newgate, leaving us standing in the way of others struggling along the road.

Mark Ashton came out to help us.

"Come in," he said, taking hold of one of our bags. Will shouldered the bale of bedding and I took the bundle of clothes and we went inside.

Jane Catlin found us storage space. "Several families slept here last night," she said, "but people begin to grow fearful, the fire is spreading so fast. Gerard Palmer has gone to see about hiring carts in case we need to move out."

"Where to?" I asked.

"To the fields. They say Moorfields and Finsbury Fields are filling up already."

When we left, Will said, "I must go to the bookshop."

For a moment I thought he was mad, thinking to go to work as usual, but then I understood. "The fire won't come as far as Paul's Churchyard, surely?"

"It's already at Queenhithe, and moving north. And the stock will take hours to shift. If we leave it too late…"

"Where would we take it?"

"I don't know. There's Stationers' Hall at Ludgate. But I need to ask Edmund. Come with me, Su, and we'll open up, and see what other booksellers are doing, and then I'll go and find Edmund."

We went to Rachel's on our way, and found her packing Tabitha's clothes and baby things in a basket.

"I don't want to leave," she said, "but if Friends decide the Bull and Mouth is unsafe I'll go too."

"To thy mother's?"

"Yes."

I exchanged a look of sympathy with her.

"At least it will be safe," she said, "outside the wall."

We left soon after and found Edmund already at the bookshop. I was relieved, for I had not wanted Will to leave me and go back along Cheapside through the crowds and alarm to Throgmorton Street.

"Will! Susanna!" Edmund was already stacking books. "This is a grim day. Is your home safe? Have you removed to the meeting house?"

He, it seemed, had left his servants packing as

much of his furniture and goods as could be got into two carts he had managed to procure – "at thirty pounds apiece," he said, "that would have been three pounds yesterday. But it must be done. The family will go to Essex, to their cousins. I'll follow on after, if the worst comes and the house be burnt. First we must see to the books." He sighed. "It's such a little time since we set them all anew on the shelves."

"Where shall we take them?" asked Will.

"To St Faith's, in Paul's crypt. It's the booksellers' church, and nearer and more fireproof, I think, than Stationers' Hall."

"But will they allow us into Faith's? Dissenters?"

"If we pay, yes. There is a storage fee that all must pay. Now, here are the instructions: bundles to be small enough for a man to lift easily, wrapped and tied, each bundle clearly marked *Martell*…"

We were soon at work. The men lifted and stacked the books while I wrapped and cut the twine and marked the parcels. It was tiring work, even though I was not lifting, and both men urged me to rest; so after an hour or two, when my hands were sore from the twine, I poured beer and looked into the basket of food Edmund had brought for us to share.

I found meat and fine bread, cheese, and apples from his garden, and a large pie of beef and spices that his cook must have baked the day before.

I cut up the pie, and we ate it from paper instead of plates, and felt great satisfaction both in the food and in our continuing work, even though outside all was panic and distress.

We had a small cart of James Martell's in the backyard of the shop, and this we loaded up with book parcels. Will and Edmund made several trips to Faith's while I continued to wrap and tie.

I felt tired, but not much more than usual. I was only four months gone with child, and my belly did not yet show my condition to the world, although I could see and feel that I had thickened a little. Rachel had told me I must wait another month or so before I felt the child move.

Each time Will and Edmund came back they spoke more of the heat and the blinding smoke.

People fleeing from the fire came into the shop to talk and shelter. They told us the fire seemed to have a will of its own, breaking out on a sudden where none had been before.

"They're saying it's a popish plot," one said.

And it seemed everyone was inclined to blame the Catholics, believing them to be in league with the French and Dutch, and that their agents were going about throwing fireballs into shops and houses and starting new fires all over the city.

Edmund was sceptical of this, convinced that the

wind and the dry timbers were to blame. When a Friend came in and told us that the fire was sweeping north up Gracechurch Street I saw that he was alarmed. He had left his family at home, helping the servants to pack.

It was midday and we were more than half finished.

"I'll go and see how things stand at home," he said. "If they are ready, I'll send them on their way, then come back to you."

Soon after he left, Mark Ashton and Gerard Palmer from the Bull and Mouth meeting arrived and told us that Friends did not feel safe staying at the tavern another night. A large number of the meeting – women with children, the elderly, and any whose businesses were now secure – were about to leave through Aldersgate in several carts. Our goods could be put aboard if we wished to leave with them.

"Where will you go?" asked Will.

"A Friend named Sylvester Wharton has a farm a mile or so out, south-east of Islington. There are barns and fields where we may camp. But he says make haste, because all the fields north of London are filling with people and he will not keep space for us if others are in need. We go with some who know the way, but Sylvester will fly a green flag from the roof so that any who come later may find the place."

Will turned to me. "Thou should go, Susanna. I'll come later, when we are finished here."

"What?" I'd no intention of leaving him. We would not be separated again; I was determined of that. "I won't go without thee!" I said. "We'll finish our work here, and go together."

"That will take two hours at least, even if Edmund is soon back."

"Then I'll help thee, and it will be done the sooner. I won't leave thee, Will."

I saw Will's face set firm. He means to overrule me, I thought, but I will not endure it.

He turned to Gerard Palmer. "Can she ride on a cart? Will there be room?"

"Yes, of course. We'll make room for such as Susanna, and for children and the sick." He looked kindly at me. "We can take thee now, Friend Susanna."

"No," I said. "No, I thank thee. I'll stay till the shop is cleared."

Will put a hand on my arm. "Susanna, I insist—"

"I will not go!" I sprang away from him. Tears stung my eyes, but they were half of rage. My voice rose. "Don't ask me to leave thee! I will not go!"

Our Friends looked embarrassed, and Will's face darkened. He pulled me with him into the back room, pushed the door to, and said in a low, angry voice,

"Do not brawl with me in public! It is unseemly—"

"I care not if it is! I won't leave without thee!"

"There is danger—"

"If there's danger we'll share it."

He seized me by the shoulders. "Thou'll do as I say! Su, thou'rt carrying our child! When my mother was in like condition my father protected her. She did not run around like a peasant. I won't have it!"

He is his father's son after all, I thought. And I retorted, "Thy mother was a lady. And I *am* a peasant."

"My mother was a farmer's daughter, as thou know. And thou'rt no peasant. Oh, Su" – he put his arms around me but I stiffened against him, resentful of his assumption of power – "let's not quarrel, love. I want thee and our child to be safe. Our Friends are waiting. Go with them. If thou go, thou can make sure our goods are aboard, and can find us shelter, perhaps in a barn. And I'll come. Tonight. I promise."

He was right. I knew it. And I knew I must give way in the end. But my heart was against it. I had such fear for him: of the fire itself, the desperate crowds, the great mass of people at the gates.

I made a last stand. "They say thousands are fleeing. We'll never find each other again!"

"Of course we will. Friends will help us."

"I don't want to leave thee," I said. But my voice was small now; he knew he'd won.

Aldersgate was jammed with carts. From my perch, high on our foremost cart, wedged in among bales of bedding, I could see soldiers ahead struggling to control the crowds, but could not understand why the queue of carts was moving so slowly. We had been stuck for nearly an hour, I reckoned.

"It's the carts coming in," said Jane Catlin, who sat near me.

We learned that there were almost as many coming in as out – large numbers of them country people with carts for hire, seeking to profit from the emergency.

But those fleeing should have right of way, I thought.

Another cart ahead of us passed through, and we jolted forward in an encouraging way. Then a wagon turned over. Children, dogs, beds and furniture spilled into the road. People began shouting, and the soldiers intervened to break up a fight while others righted the vehicle. And all the time hot, choking smoke swept over us on the gale, full of dust and ash, and we found our clothes covered in it, our eyes and throats burning. A rumble of thunder overhead startled me. Was it true thunder, or the roar of collapsing buildings? We could not tell, but the sound was fearsome.

When at last we made our way through the gate there were more narrow streets to delay us. And now carts were turning off, or emerging from lanes into the flow of traffic, or stopping to unload. Our own carts stopped once or twice, and several of our people left, to go to friends or relations who lived outside the walls.

I had already lost the company of Rachel. She had gone to her mother's house in Houndsditch, travelling with other Friends who had relations east of the city. I knew how unwilling she was. "I'd rather stay with Friends – even in a field," she'd said, when we met up again at the Bull and Mouth. "But my mother will fear the worst if Tabby and I don't appear. Come with me, Su! There'll be room for thee. And thou shouldn't sleep out."

But I would not go. Will would look for me at Sylvester Wharton's, and Houndsditch was far from there.

We resumed our journey, and now the tight-packed houses gave way to more isolated farms and cottages. The air was clearer, though the sky all around was hidden by dark clouds streaming west. The wind was hot and heavy with ash. My dress and the bales of bedding in the cart were by now covered in a layer of debris: fragments of paper, parchment, linen, plaster – the very stuff of people's lives. I looked back and saw the city ablaze under dense black smoke with flames leaping in it, and thought with terror of Will; and I believe that if I could have got down then and fought my way back to him through the crowds I would have done so.

Jane Catlin seemed to guess my thoughts. She touched my hand. "Better to look forward," she said, indicating the road ahead, "and trust in God. See, there is the green flag."

And indeed we had reached Sylvester Wharton's farm. I was glad to be helped down from the cart and to stretch and move, and to feel grass under my feet and breathe cleaner air.

Then I looked around, and was amazed. As far as I could see in every direction – from Islington all the way back to London – the fields were full of people; I had not known there *were* so many people in London. Some had put up tents; others sat in the shelter of a cart, or had a horse tethered near by; but most had simply a few possessions piled beside them on the ground. Rich and poor together, all were homeless. There were children and dogs running about, and babies crying, and a great hubbub of thousands of voices, so loud and continuous that it seemed to be the voice of the earth itself.

A grey-haired man I took to be Sylvester Wharton greeted us all and began advising us where to go.

Gerard Palmer took charge of me and my bedding, and he and another Friend carried them to a sheltered place in the lee of a hedge. There we erected a makeshift tent of propped branches and a blanket, and I laid my bedding inside and reckoned Will and I would be snug enough at night. Some people chose to sleep in the carts and guard the goods, while others – the sick, and those with young children, or women who were near their time – were in the house and barns. I was glad to be outside, where Will and I could be together. Now, in late afternoon, the wind was strong but warm, and I did not fear the cold.

We all looked back at the city. I remembered how I'd seen it from Islington last year with the cloud of kites hanging above it. Now a much greater cloud hung there, glowing red beneath, with flashes of flame erupting from it. Somewhere a steeple blazed like a torch, and of a sudden we heard several explosions, one after the other, and a ripple of panic went through the crowd like the wind through grass. I heard cries of "Invasion!" and "The Hollanders!" and my heartbeat quickened.

But Gerard Palmer said, "They are blowing up buildings to halt the fire. It should have been done before."

Elizabeth Wright gazed on the scene almost with satisfaction. "It is God's judgement," she said. "God's terrible judgement on us all. Nothing can save the city now."

I didn't want to listen to such talk. It filled me with dread. I stared back down the road. Without a cart to manoeuvre, Will should have passed through Aldersgate easily. He could not be far behind us, surely? But among all the people walking and riding along the way I did not see him.

Those Friends who organized our departure had brought supplies of food, and soon cooking smells were carried on the wind. Two cauldrons were in use, one in Sylvester Wharton's kitchen and a larger one over a fire in the yard. I saw that there were few fires lit in the fields. Perhaps the people were mostly too close-packed, or too afraid of the very sight of fire. Indeed, the sound of the bonfire in the farmyard, its greedy crackling and sparking, frightened rather than drew me.

And I had no interest in food. It was evening, and still I waited for Will.

Faintly, from Islington to the north, we heard steeple-house bells ringing. And from London too: but that was a reverse peel, a warning of fire still spreading. It was impossible, from here, to see which streets were ablaze and which still safe, but the endless line of people moving along the road brought news. The fire had reached Lombard Street and Cornhill. The pipes and cisterns were all dry; there was no water to fight the fire. Late in the day came news that the Exchange had burned. I recalled that sumptuous place with its colonnades and the candlelit shops glowing in the dusk and the smell of spices. I could not believe it was no longer there.

"Burnt to the ground," a woman said. Her face was scorched red, her eyelashes gone.

"We had ado to get out," her husband told us. "Burning timbers all across the road. Blocked our way. We turned down Kemp's Passage —"

"Black as Hell, it was, and smoke blinding you —"

"Found ourselves didn't know where, fire all around…"

Slowly, interrupting each other, they told us how they had found their way at last to Aldersgate and escaped. And all the time I was thinking of Will, imagining him trapped in Paul's Churchyard, ringed round with fire.

I stared towards London. Paul's still stood. When the smoke shifted I could see it. But where was Will? Why didn't he come? If these folk had got out, why couldn't he? I felt angry – furious with him for sending me away, and with myself for going.

The day darkened early, the sun hidden behind a haze of smoke. People began settling down for the night.

"Susanna, thou must eat," said Jane Catlin. She brought me a bowl of stew, but I had no appetite. I sipped a little, then gave the bowl to someone else and went to stand by the roadside, looking out for Will.

It was hard to distinguish faces in the dusk. The flow of people had lessened, and at last it almost stopped.

Jane took my arm. "Come away now, Susanna. Think of thy child."

I did, and saw it fatherless, Will caught in the maze of burning alleyways, overcome by smoke, never to find his way out. "He said he'd come. He promised."

"He'll have gone to shelter somewhere. He'll come in the morning, never fear."

But I was besieged by fear. As night fell we saw before us the full horror of the burning city, lit up in its own dreadful day, and heard the roar of its destruction. All around us people sobbed and prayed.

"I'm London born and bred," said Jane. "Those streets – I knew them all." And she wept for her city.

The wind had turned cool.

"Come and sleep with me and Elizabeth Wright," said Jane. "Thou'll be warmer."

"No, I thank thee."

He would surely not come now, not in the dark, but I wanted to be in my own shelter, to keep a place for him there, in case by chance he did. I curled up, pulling the blankets close around me, but I could not sleep. I was too full of fearful imaginings.

William

I worked alone for an hour after Susanna left, stacking and baling. Outside, the street was full of people and carts, streaming towards the gates in a great clamour and confusion. There were explosions, rumbles of thunder; I knew the fire must still be spreading. Perhaps Edmund would be unable to get back. And Susanna: I'd been overbearing with her, and was sorry, and we'd parted unhappily. I longed to be done with the books, to go and find her.

The shop door opened, and Nat came in. I was never more glad to see him.

"We're finished at the print shop," he said. "Made safe all we can. I thought thou might need help."

"I do," I said gratefully. "Edmund has gone to see to his goods and family, and Susanna with Friends to find shelter in the fields. She didn't want to go, Nat, but I insisted. We quarrelled."

"She'll forgive thee." His words, casually spoken, cheered me more than he could have imagined. He began tying parcels as I wrapped them. "And thou did right to send her. I hear the gates are almost blocked with traffic now. They've had to ban carts from coming in, to ease the flow. You've got a good pile of books here. Faith's is near full, they say."

"Help me get another cartload there, will you? I don't know when Edmund will be back."

"For sure."

We loaded up, and wheeled the cart the short distance to the storage place. Faith's was a church within a church, in the crypt of Paul's, and the books had to be carried down the steps to be taken from us by a verger and stacked within. We took it in turns to transport a few parcels while the other one guarded the cart, which we feared would otherwise be stolen.

I went with the first load, and saw how full the space now was. It no longer resembled a place of worship but was filling from floor to ceiling with books and papers – booksellers and stationers coming and going all the while with more stock. I thought of all the cellars and repositories through-out London that must be the same: the Guildhall, the company halls, the strongrooms at the Tower; and all the steeple-houses filled with the furniture and goods of their parishioners.

When Nat and I returned from our second delivery, Edmund was back – his hands and clothes dusty and streaks of soot on his face. He was grateful to have Nat's help and apologized to me for being so long.

"They are all gone now, on their way to Essex," he said, "and the servants with them, except Martin, who will travel with me. Think well, you two, before you burden yourselves with more goods than you need. It was impossible to get everything aboard and a cause of much argument what should go and what should stay."

I wondered whether the virginal had gone; and I thought of Catherine, and of the Ramsey home and all its fine rooms under threat.

"I met Nick Barron," Edmund told me. "He says he is ruined – his warehouse burnt, his home now in the path of the fire."

I was shocked. For both my father and me, Nicholas Barron had represented security, wealth and advancement. He was to have been the making of me. It did not seem possible that such a man could be ruined.

"Could he save nothing?" I asked.

"Only such gold as he could carry. The rest he's buried, and left to chance, as I have. The great stock of silks is in strongboxes in the cellars, but he has little hope of its survival. And he has no reserves. He put everything into the business, and last year the plague cut his trade to the bone."

He'd be camping in the fields, then, I thought, as no doubt many once prosperous men were; would perhaps go back to Shropshire, if he had relatives there. It must be the end of all his dreams. I pitied him; having less, I could not lose so much.

We finished our work and took the last load to Faith's, which we were told would be sealed shut so that no fire could enter. It was now late afternoon, I guessed, although all sense of time had gone. I thought of Susanna waiting for me, and felt impatient to be away.

The city was a threatening place now. The three of us decided to stay together while we could. We went first to Nat's lodgings. Being reluctant to leave the cart, we took it with us to Creed Lane, where Nat found the Corders already fled. He put his few clothes and a bundle of bedding into the cart, and we made our way back to Paul's and along Paternoster Row.

Edmund needed to go home, where Martin waited with horses, and then the two of them would go out through Bishopsgate to take the Woodford road. Nat and I had planned to leave through Aldersgate, but the street was blocked all the way back. Edmund waited with us as we debated what to do. All around us people were shouting, arguing, exchanging news. Someone spread an alarm that the authorities were about to shut the gates, causing a wave of panic to run through the crowd, which was unable to move forward or back.

"They want citizens to stay and fight the fire."

"It's too late for that!"

A push started; someone fell and went under the crush of feet; others screamed.

The thought of the gates closing, the city locking us into its fiery heart, terrified me. But then we heard that the ban was only on carts coming in. We did not know what to believe.

"Come with me," Edmund suggested. "You might get out sooner by Moorgate or Bishopsgate."

We agreed, and followed him.

Now we were moving east, into the wind and smoke. We passed the top of Bow Lane, and I looked down towards the steeple-house of Mary Aldermary, and saw beyond it a towering wall of flame. People were fleeing, bursting out of lanes and alleys, carrying bundles, children, even furniture. We heard the voice of the fire – a vast roar, so loud it made normal speech impossible – and within that sound was a malicious hungry crackling. The heat scorched my face; my eyes stung and my throat was full of burning ash.

As we hurried along Poultry the smoke parted to reveal a great building all ablaze, flames leaping from its roof. I realized it was the Exchange, and I stared in fascination and horror.

Men were there with water squirts, pumping, but they shouted that the water carried no force; it was almost gone. And their efforts were wasted: the building was doomed. We could not see its frontage, but fire was spouting from the upper storeys and balconies. Then, as we watched, the flames turned strange colours – blue, purple and green – and a wondrous smell of spices spread all around.

"The storerooms below," said Edmund. And I realized that he himself must have had a stock of spices stored there, and that it was his wealth, or part of it, that burned so deliciously: cinnamon, nutmeg, cloves, anise.

The fire began to leap and invade the nearby houses and shops. We turned off, up a narrow lane – I had lost my bearings, but Edmund knew this area. The lane was full of people, a few still hauling goods out of their houses, struggling with babies, children, even a sick man on a pallet. Nat pulled the cart while I pushed from behind and Edmund walked alongside us. The cart, jolting over uneven ground, struck hard against a stone; a book (Nat's Bible, I think) bounced out, and Edmund stooped to retrieve it. He straightened up – and at that moment the house next to him erupted in flame, fire shooting from the windows, the whole structure lit up in an instant.

People screamed, turned, fled back towards Poultry. As the house blazed, isolated from its untouched neighbours, a man – red-faced and frantic – pointed at Edmund. "He threw something! A fireball! I saw him take it from his cart!"

Edmund began to protest, but to my horror the red-faced man struck and felled him with one blow from his fist.

The others surrounded Nat and me.

"They're Quakers or some such! Didn't you hear them talking?"

But even as they went to set about us there was a cry of "Fire! Fire!" and I looked up to see a nearby roof and jetty blazing. The whole overhanging structure broke away and fell, showering us all with burning debris.

It was enough to scatter our attackers – though one had the forethought to take our cart with him. The lane was full of black, choking smoke and the burning house was now well alight.

Edmund struggled to his feet.

"Quickly!" I said.

Nat and I helped him away. He was shocked and in pain, and I feared his nose might be broken. One eye was closed, the flesh around it darkening and swelling. Despite this, he was able to direct us another way to his home. We hurried, guiding him between us, pushing through crowds until we came out in Throgmorton Street and I recognized with relief the Ramsey house.

Edmund's servant, the young groom Martin, cried out in alarm when he saw his master. He led us into the kitchen and ran to fetch water and cloths.

"Lucky not everything has gone to Essex," he said, producing soap and a bowl. Nat made a cold compress for the eye and told me to hold it in place while he bathed the bloody nose. Edmund submitted to this, gently apologizing for the trouble.

"It's no trouble," I said – though in truth it was keeping me from Susanna, and I saw now that the day was more advanced than I'd thought, and growing dark.

Martin found food that had been left behind for Edmund's journey to Essex: bread, cheese and beer. He advised his master not to leave that night. "I went up to Bishopsgate a while back to look around. There's a great press of people. And it's almost dark;

roads'll be unsafe. We'll do better to leave early tomorrow."

Edmund nodded, cautiously feeling his nose. "But the fire? If it spreads this way…"

We were terrifyingly close to the burning Exchange – only the width of a street or two separated us. Selfishly I wanted Edmund to say it was too dangerous, that we must go now. I was desperate to reach Susanna before night; I'd promised her.

Nat looked at me. He knew what I wanted. "It'll be dark even before we get through the gate," he said.

He was right. And we couldn't go blundering across unlit fields in search of our friends. We had to wait somewhere till morning, and it might as well be here.

Edmund got to his feet and looked out. "We can leave at once if the fire comes too close. Are the horses ready?"

"Been ready an hour or more," said Martin.

Edmund turned to us. "But you – Will? Nat?"

"We'll stay," I said.

Edmund touched his battered face again. He moved awkwardly, stiff from his fall. "Do we have willow bark, Martin? Any herbs? And is there bedding left here? Though I doubt we'll sleep much…"

* * *

I slept hardly at all. Nat and I shared an unmade bed in the girls' chamber, which had been cleared of all their possessions. We folded our coats under our heads for pillows, drew the curtains around the bed but opened a window to cool the room, for the night would have been hot even if it were not for the fire raging outside. The sound of the fire was a background roar, louder now it was night, against which we heard sudden explosions, the rush and splintering of collapsing buildings, the cries of people still out in the streets. Somewhere near by a dog howled relentlessly.

After an hour or so I got up and went to the open window, which faced south, and saw the city bright as day.

It's unstoppable, I thought; only a matter of time before all is consumed.

I went back to bed and lay thinking of Susanna, pictured her lying awake, like me, fearing for me as she watched the city burn.

I must have slept at last. I woke to a banging on the door, and Martin's voice, urgent. "Sirs! We must go! The fire's upon us!"

We sprang up and ran to the window. One of the houses opposite had caught. Its roof was ablaze, flames shooting upwards into the darkness. The street was packed with people rushing, crying out, hastening towards Bishopsgate Street.

"We'll leave by the back gate."

Martin had brought the horses into the yard: two of them, for Edmund and himself. Edmund looked pale, his left eye half closed, swollen and purple, his nose blackened with bruising. Martin led us down a narrow series of paths that ran alongside a great steeple-house and past the walled garden of a grand house. Priests in black robes came out of the steeple-house, arms and handcarts full of hastily wrapped bundles, and went hurrying along ahead of us. We emerged through a small gateway opposite London Wall, and there we saw people already crowding towards the gates.

"You two had best go through Moorgate, if you can," Edmund said.

It was time to part. We wished one another God-speed, not knowing when we'd meet again. Edmund cast one regretful look back at his home, then he and Martin left us, and Nat and I moved to join the crowd at Moorgate.

We knew that dawn was breaking only because there was a yellow tinge to the dense layer of smoke blowing over us on the wind. The sun was not visible. We heard from voices around us that Cheapside was on fire, the Post Office gone, and the *Gazette*'s offices, and Mary le Bow. Baynard's Castle, that great stronghold on the river, had blazed all night and was now a ruin. People looked dazed and bewildered. We shuffled, all of us, towards the gate, and passed through into Moorfields.

Those fields, which a few days before had been pleasure gardens, laid out with walks and shrubs, were now full of homeless citizens and their piles of belongings, their babies, children, dogs, their crated chickens, even their pigs. We walked among them, trying to keep our bearings, to head north-west, but without sun or light we had little sense of direction, and had constantly to step aside to avoid huddled families. We could not see more than a few yards in the smoky darkness, but as we walked on we became aware of people all around us, in one vast encampment, coughing, groaning, crying, arguing. Many were just beginning to stir after the night, but hundreds more were on the move, all the paths clogged with the slow tide of refuge seekers.

And somewhere among all these was Susanna. Only now did I realize how long it might take me to find her.

Susanna

I woke to the sound of someone pissing into the hedge near by; heard him sigh in relief and move off. Instinctively, eyes still shut, I reached out, but the space beside me was empty. I was cold, and hungry, and the ground was hard under my hip bone; but none of these things would have mattered if Will had been with me.

I opened my eyes. It was dawn – or rather, it was no longer night. The sun was hidden behind a thick yellow-brown mass of smoke and cloud that covered all the sky.

I stood up, chafing my upper arms to get warm. All around, people had begun to stir and rise – and all of us looked towards London.

The fire still raged. We heard its roar, and here and there we saw flashes of flame as a spire or tall building caught light. The smoke borne to us on the wind was laden with blackened fragments and burning embers. People stared, some in horror-struck silence, many weeping.

"It is the end of the world!" a woman cried out, and fell to her knees. And Elizabeth Wright saw God's righteous anger in it, and said there would be no end to the suffering till London was utterly destroyed.

I moved away from Elizabeth and went to tidy myself and to piss behind the hedge. I needed to go more often these days; Rachel said it was the babe growing inside me, pressing down. I put a hand on my belly; it was no longer quite flat. Will's child was growing.

Will. I saw that the movement of people along the road had begun again, and hope sprang up in me that he had perhaps stopped somewhere nearer the city wall when it grew dark, and would soon be here. I shook out my crumpled skirts, took a comb from the pocket under my gown, tidied my hair, and fastened my cap in place. I'd been wearing the same linen since first-day, and had not washed since then, except to splash my face with cold water before we left Bow Lane. No matter. He would be dirty too.

Jane Catlin saw me and said there was milk at the farmhouse; that I should come. I followed her, and waited my turn for a bowl of new milk, creamy and warm from the cow. It was like being at home in Long Aston. And I thought: if my mother could see me now...

There was bread too, and I took a piece and went to stand once more by the roadside, looking for Will.

Three hours I reckon I waited, maybe four. I grew weary, and sat down on a tussock, but would not leave the road. My hope, which had been so strong at dawn, slowly shrivelled and died. If he had left through Aldersgate yesterday he should have been here by now. The fear that he had come to some harm grew in me.

"He may have lost the way, nothing more," Jane had said. But he'd been given directions, the way was straight enough, and the green flag still flew. Jane was kind, but I longed for Rachel, or Nat – and most of all for Will. Once or twice I saw someone who looked kindly, and ran and asked after Will, or after the booksellers at Faith's. No one had news of them, but I heard that the fire had broken all bounds, that Cheapside and the Guildhall were aflame, the wall breached at Ludgate, the city doomed, and folk fleeing through all the northern gates.

Where *was* he? I raged against him in my heart, remembering how he'd sent me away. I should have stayed, faced danger with him. Anything would have been better than this waiting.

I was in the thick of such thoughts when I became aware of women's voices calling my name. "Susanna Heywood? Hast seen Susanna Heywood?"

I sprang up, my heart leaping. He was here! He was asking for me! All my fear and anger vanished in an instant. I ran back into the yard, where the voices came from – and stopped short in bitter disappointment. The man who stood there with his back to me was not Will.

And now my alarm increased, for I saw that this man was not a homeless Londoner at all, but someone from outside that chaos: clean, well dressed, with an air of authority; a man of middle age who had travelled here with a servant and horses.

My mouth went dry. He has come with bad news, I thought; I don't want to hear it.

Then the man turned towards me, and I saw that he was Will's father.

Henry Heywood looked at me, uncertainly at first, as if he was doubtful that he'd recognized me aright, and then he said, "Susanna ... Heywood?"

"Yes," I said, trembling.

He frowned. "Are you here alone? Where is my son?"

So Will was not found? His father knew nothing? "I don't know!" I exclaimed. "I hoped thou'd tell me! He said he'd come without fail last night but he never did, and I've waited here all morning and no news of him. I don't know where he is!"

To my shame I began to cry. The tears welled up and would not be stopped. I hated to be seen like this, by Henry Heywood of all people – this man before whom I'd always wanted to appear strong, certain, even defiant. And now I was sobbing like a child and conscious of my dirty, crumpled condition and how I must smell and what a foolish slut he must think me.

I sniffed and wiped my eyes. I was surprised to see that he had come closer and his expression had changed to one of concern. "Please," he begged, "please, my dear, don't distress yourself. We'll find him, never fear. Come…"

He led me inside the farm kitchen and asked the maidservant for a chair for me and a glass of beer – for all the world as if it were his home and not a stranger's. And the girl obeyed him.

I sipped my beer and said, "I'm sorry. I'd hoped so much – when I heard my name called…"

A silence fell between us, and I knew we were both thinking that we shared a name now, and I wondered how he felt about that.

"Thou had my letter?" I ventured.

"I did."

He looked at me, at my face and body, and I knew

he was looking at my belly, and I said, "The child will be born at the end of January."

He nodded. "I read your letter many times. I did not know what to think of it, what to believe, what to do. I decided, at last, to go to London."

He sighed and shook his head. "This is a great catastrophe."

I did not know whether he meant the destruction of London or my marriage to his son, and so said nothing.

He turned to me. "What was Will doing, yesterday? What caused you to separate?"

I explained about the books. "He sent me away. I didn't want to go."

"He was right to do so," he said. And his tone told me that he thought it had been my duty to obey.

I said, in a small voice, "All I want is to find him."

"And we *will* find him!" His voice was kind, reassuring, and I saw that he liked me better like this, tearful and womanly, as he saw it. "I'll ride to Aldersgate; make enquiries. If he is out of the city, I'll find him. I have my man with me; we'll go together. But you" – he looked at me sternly – "you will wait here."

He sounded so confident, so sure of getting people to do his bidding and answer his questions, that I *was* reassured, and I warmed to him for the first time. It was comforting to be in the care of such a man.

"We'll go now," he said, "while you rest and eat. I'll tell the girl to fetch you something—"

"No!" I cried. "Do not! There are many here in need – some sick, or with babes..."

But he was up and away, summoning the maid as he left, and sending her off to fetch bread and bacon.

He had not been gone five minutes, the maid not yet returned, when I heard from outside loud voices and exclamations – one of them the voice I'd been waiting for.

"Will!"

I jumped up, and ran outside. He was there, in the yard, he and his father standing a few paces apart. Each of them looked wary, as if unwilling to be the first to move closer.

"Will!" I cried out again.

He turned to me. I raced across the yard and into his arms, unmindful of folk around us looking on, and Will caught and hugged me and kissed me hard, and hugged me again, and then stood with my hand clasped in his, facing his father.

William

When I came into Sylvester Wharton's yard and saw my father there, I was at first so astonished that I thought I must be mistaken, or having delusions. But I saw him recognize me. He shouted in surprise, and I cried out too, my voice cracking from the smoke in my lungs. I sprang towards him and then, remembering the coldness between us, fell back, uncertain what to do or say.

Susanna, flying to my arms, spared me the decision. Now, with her hand in mine, I saw that my father's expression was not hostile; indeed, he appeared to be on the brink of tears.

"Will! My boy!" he said – and I let go Susanna's hand and ran into his embrace, and we held each other close and wept.

"It has been too long," he said. "And the fault is mine. I should have written to you."

We broke apart, and I began to cough, hoarsely apologizing: "I'm covered in ash ... dirty..."

"No matter." He held out a hand to Susanna, bringing the three of us together.

"You must come to the inn," he said. "You can't sleep in the fields. I am lodged at the Angel. It's not far, and I have horses."

"But, Father, how came thou here? At this time?" I asked, between fits of coughing. "What brought thee?"

I saw him wince at my "thee" and "thou", but he let them pass.

"Your wife wrote to me."

"My wife...?" I turned to Susanna.

She looked me in the eye, defiant. "I told your father of our marriage and asked him to forgive thee," she said.

"Thou *wrote*? And didn't tell me?" I was astonished and a little annoyed – and I saw my father frown in disapproval.

"I made up my mind to come," he said. "Not to write first and arrange it, but to come and see..." – he paused, and glanced, embarrassed, at Susanna – "how the land lay. We reached Islington on Sunday afternoon, and heard reports of a big fire spreading on the river front, but we were in time to find room at the Angel before people began flooding out of the city."

"Thou did not enter the city?"

"No. By Sunday night I knew that would be unwise. Instead, I looked for you in the fields. All day yesterday Ned and I were up and down the fields, making enquiries. We came across several groups of Quakers. Very civil, most of them, and willing to help – though coarse in their outward manner, as all those people are. This morning I was told there were more Quakers at Wharton's Farm, so I came here – and found your wife."

He took Susanna's arm – a gentlemanly gesture which startled her, I noticed with amusement. "You must come to the Angel," he said. "You shall have my bed and I'll sleep downstairs—"

"No, Father!"

"I insist! I have a large room. We may eat together in private. It's a busy place, an excellent hostelry, warm, good food. You would not have your wife spend another night in the fields?"

He was leading us towards the stables, where we found Ned waiting with the horses.

I had not seen Ned for four years, and the sight of him reminded me sharply of home and the battles I'd had with my father, when I'd been sent to eat in the kitchen with Ned and the other servants. We greeted each other warmly, and then Ned turned to my father. "Is it back to the inn, sir, now they are found?"

"Let me fetch a few clothes," I said.

I went with Susanna to our store in the cart, and we took out clean linen and breeches, a skirt and bodice for Susanna, and her hat.

We found Nat, who had melted into the crowd when he saw my father, and told him of our arrangements. We promised to meet soon. When we returned to the yard Ned offered his horse to us, but Susanna refused to ride, even as pillion.

"I have scarce ever been on a horse before," she said to me, "and I fear for the child now."

"We'll walk," I said.

And so we walked, all of us, leading the horses.

It was less than a mile to the inn. As we came into the yard Susanna and I brushed ourselves down. I was covered in a layer of ash and dust, the brim of my hat full of blackened fragments.

"Thy face is scorched," Susanna said. It felt sore. I hadn't noticed until now.

My father opened the door and a warm smell of hospitality wafted out: beer, roasting meat, new bread, rosemary, sage. I felt my appetite sharpen.

Susanna hesitated, straightening her collar, tucking in ends of hair. "I am not fit to enter this place," she whispered to me.

But my father ushered her in. "Come. Come in, daughter. You look well enough."

It was a great pleasure to be in the well-furnished room my father had secured. There was a bed of dark carved wood, hung with patterned cloth in russet and blue, and a washstand with scented soap and clean linen cloths. In the window embrasure at the far end were a table and several chairs. I looked out of the window, which faced north over fields, the road to Islington winding between them. All along the road, travellers laden with their household goods were walking or riding, and still the fields were filling with people.

Susanna and I were eager to wash, so we called for hot water, and took turns. While she was busy my father and I went downstairs, where we found the inn full – in great part with people who had fled the fire. We heard stories of loss all around.

"There was no cart to be had. All will be burnt."

"The poor little dog ran off and could not be found…"

"We hired a cart for forty pounds. They loaded up our goods – and we never saw them again. Paid forty pounds for the cart and all our goods stolen! We have nothing left…"

My father and I found a bench in a quiet corner

and drank beer and talked. We were to talk much over the next few days, but this was when I learned what Susanna had put in her letter and how it had brought my father to me.

"I never thought to have had such a letter from a woman," he said, pulling it out from under his jacket and showing it to me – though I could not see to read it since our corner was too dark. "She writes a fair hand, Will – very fair; Anne cannot write at all, and neither could your mother. But, you know, I don't like a woman to be writing. You see what it leads to: a letter like this, sent without her husband's knowledge… You must manage her better, Will."

"Father, Susanna and I had nothing but letters to sustain us for three years…"

But he brushed this aside and went on. "When I saw it was from her I was minded to burn it. You know I had no love for her; I admit it freely. But curiosity got the better of me. When I read of your marriage I was angry, and when she claimed she was with child I thought: That whore has lured him into marriage—"

"Father—"

"No! Hear me out. I won't mince words. I'd always mistrusted the wench; you know that. But then … she wrote of how much you missed your home, Will. And how she believed you and I should be reconciled. I have it here – you may read it yourself. There was a truth to it that touched my heart. I thought of your mother, and how she would have felt, knowing that I had broken with you. But then – I must tell you this, Will; do not be angry – a little doubt crept in, and I asked myself: Is the wench after my money —"

"No!"

"It came into my mind, Will. I thought: She has married him and now she means to get him back his inheritance. I talked about it with your mother – your stepmother – and she agreed I must go to London to see how things stood. Was the marriage legal? Could it be undone?"

"It cannot! Will not! I am twenty-one and —"

"I know that. Hear me out. I came here today, and met Susanna. Will" – he turned to me in a gesture of contrition – "Will, I saw at once that I was wrong, that I'd been wrong all along, that she loved you and had only your good at heart. She was not bold and scheming, as I remembered her. The poor girl was distraught – feared you were lost to her in this calamity…" He paused, and shook his head. "What will you *do*, Will? How will you live? She is carrying your child."

"We will find a way," I said. "When we wait upon God in the silence —"

"Oh, don't talk to me of that!" he exclaimed. "God is all very well but it's money you need, boy. Food in your bellies; a roof over your heads. Your lodgings are gone, I suppose?"

"I believe so. And the shop may burn too. But the stock of books is safe. We worked all day to store everything in the crypt of Paul's. No fire could get in there. We will rebuild the business."

I told him about Nicholas Barron and saw that he was shocked.

"I thought to see your future there," he said. "Well, you would have gone to another master. But I'm sorry for the man. To lose so much is a great blow."

The three of us ate together in my father's room. There was a good spread of food: beef, a mutton pie, woodcock, bread and herbs. We paused a moment to give thanks before falling to.

Susanna was somewhat subdued, I think because she felt herself to be an outsider in this reunion; but my father likes reticence in a woman, and I saw that he approved of her quietness. She was pretty, too, in her brown dress that matched her eyes, a few curls of hair damp on her neck. I saw that he was warming to her. He asked after her parents, and whether they missed her, and what trade her brother was in. He was at his most charming – but he could afford to be, I thought; he was away from his home town and his status as an alderman. Would he welcome her into the heart of his family in Hemsbury? He had said once that he never could.

I asked after Anne, who was now seventeen. She was, he said, a dutiful child, pretty and accomplished, who should marry well in due course. He talked also of his business, which flourished; of his new apprentice; and he told stories that made us laugh about the foibles of some of his customers and suppliers. It all seemed familiar, and yet remote from my life now, and I wondered if I could ever truly regain my place in the family – or even whether I wished to.

Later, as night fell, we went downstairs and out into the yard, where several dozen others were gathered, and from there gazed at the terrible sight of all London on fire. Flames seemed to be bursting through Aldersgate, and someone came running with news that Goldsmiths' Hall was destroyed, and all of Foster Lane, and the fire was advancing on Paul's.

"Nothing can halt it," the man said. "Christ Church and Newgate will be next. They'll have moved the prisoners by now."

Newgate! I thought of that hated place, and rejoiced at the vision of fire consuming it. The straw would blaze, the lice pop and crackle; the iron shackles would melt. Flames would race up the stairways and into every cell, feeding on the grime-encrusted walls, the smoke-blackened ceilings, the plague rooms where my friends had suffered, the stocks and whipping posts. The whole structure would blaze from cellar to roof, and be cleansed.

Perhaps, after all, the fire *was* from God.

But those around us were talking of plots.

"It's the papists. A papist plot. They're in league with the Dutch and French. No fire could spread so fast by accident. They planned it: strike out the water tower, the wharves; start fires here, there, all about. Confusion and chaos. Then invasion. We'll hear of invasion next, I tell you."

The talk washed over us. We were tired. Susanna went to bed, and I followed soon after. The landlord had somehow managed to find my father a small room on an upper floor, even though the inn was full; no doubt a servant or family member had been displaced.

Susanna and I lay and talked.

"Thy father has been kind," she said. "I met him once in Hemsbury; I think I told you. I sensed the light in him then, and felt pity for him."

"He has taken to *thee*." I would not tell her all his remarks about her letter, but I added, teasing, pulling her closer, "Though he thinks I should demand more obedience from thee."

We laughed and kissed.

"Thou'rt not angry that I wrote to him?"

"No. It has brought us together. But for him to arrive, now, with the city in flames! It is extraordinary that he found us."

"It is God's work, I think."

Next morning, when we went outside, I felt a change.

"The wind has dropped."

We looked at the city. The smoke pouring from it now rose straight up and formed a dense black cloud above.

This will help, I thought: the wind no longer fanning the fire. It seemed to me more than ever that I saw God's hand in these events. The fierce east wind had arisen on the night the fire started, and now that the entire city had burnt it had dropped.

The explosions continued. News came that Paul's had blazed all night. I thought of the books, sealed in the crypt of Faith's. The fire would not reach them there, no matter how hot it became.

We stayed several nights with my father at the Angel. The fire at last ceased to spread, and we saw the leaping flames die to a red glow and then to a view of blackened walls and ruined buildings. Few dared go back at first. Those who did reported stones too hot to walk on, fires still burning in crypts and cellars.

One night an alarm went up: the French and Dutch were invading. We heard men yelling, "Arm! Arm!" and saw a great surge of people towards the city. But it was all false, and the trained bands were sent in to restore order. Next day the King was seen at Moorfields speaking to the people and assuring them that the fire was an accident and not the work of agitators or traitors. Soldiers came with tents and shelters for those in need, and set up places where people could go for the food and drink which had been requisitioned from the countryside around. We were glad to be at the Angel, but I went most days to meet our Friends at Sylvester Wharton's. On fifth-day Nat was not there; I heard he had gone to Houndsditch to ask after Rachel and her family. When I reported this to Susanna she smiled and said, "Nat has a fondness for Rachel."

"Thou think so?"

"I'm sure of it. Oh, I doubt she knows yet; her heart is full of Vincent. But she likes Nat, and he will wait…"

It was seventh-day, almost a week after the fire began, when Susanna and I went with my father to see the ruined city.

The sight was worse than anything I had imagined. From the ruins of Cheapside we could see the river; scarcely a wall now stood in our view.

Edmund's house in Throgmorton Street was burnt to the ground, only part of the garden remaining, full of ash and scorched timbers. Smoke still rose from the rubble and the ground was hot underfoot. We tried to walk to Bow Lane, but it was difficult to find familiar streets – all was one mass of destruction, with here and there a ruined wall, a broken tower. Around us people picked their way over the smouldering embers.

We came at last upon the ruins of Mary Aldermary. Several walls were still standing but the tower that had shaded our window was burnt to its base. The house we lived in had been built of wood. Nothing remained, and the attic space where we had been so happy was now empty sky.

Paul's was still a landmark, and we made our way towards it, walking over solidified streams of lead from the roof which had melted and poured down the streets.

Our shop was gone. I had believed that Faith's would still be secure, but my trust in that stronghold was misplaced. When the great tower collapsed, it seemed the walls and ceilings had fallen in, breaking open stone tombs and sending them crashing through the roof of the crypt.

Several booksellers and stationers were gathered there, searching among the debris. One of them saw me approaching and said, "You'll find no books here. Nothing but ashes." Another told me that St Faith's had burned all night and everything within had been destroyed. "My entire stock," he said. "My business. I don't know what I'll do."

"There is scarcely a book left in London," a scholarly old man said. His clothes were grey with dust and his eyes full of sadness. "Shops, libraries, schools, churches – all are gone."

And my work with it, I realized. Edmund was not yet here, but his efforts, I knew, would now be directed towards rebuilding his home and his spice business. Once again I was without work – along with thousands of others.

My father understood this. That evening at the inn, while Susanna rested upstairs, he said to me, "You must both come back with me to Hemsbury for a while – at least till the child is born. You can't live without home or income."

Instinctively I rejected this suggestion. I did not want to go home, to be in his power again.

"You won't want Quakers – fanatics – in your house."

"I want my son, and my grandchild. And if others speak ill of you, they will not dare do so to my face."

It was a generous gesture from him – for I knew

how much he valued his status in Hemsbury and how fragile such status could be. But we could not go.

"Friends will help us," I said. "Friends in Mile End and Southwark and other places outside the city walls." I mustered a more powerful argument. "And I would not let Susanna travel in her condition. She cannot ride, and to travel by carrier is slow and hard. It might endanger the child."

He nodded. "Perhaps you are right. Then I'll give you money. I have some with me, and will send more—"

"No, Father. There is no need. I have savings." I patted my hip, where I kept a purse well hidden.

"Then keep them! They won't last long."

"No."

I could not explain to him why I was so unwilling to accept his help when I would take it gladly from Friends. It seemed to me like weakness, like defeat. And I would never admit defeat to him.

"Will," he said, "you can't afford to be proud. You have no work, no home. You have lost everything."

"I have my wife and child," I said, "and the love of God."

He sighed in exasperation. "But how will you *live*, boy?"

❖   ❖   ❖

On first-day morning Susanna and I went to the farm again, and Friends gathered in a field and waited on God in silence. A light rain had begun to fall – the first in months. All around us, in the fields, others were at prayer, or walking to churches in Islington. It was only a week since the fire began, and all our lives were utterly changed. I knew I had to answer my father's question, and soon. How *would* we live?

That night I talked to Susanna.

"My father wants to give us money."

"He told me. I thanked him for his kindness."

"Thou thanked him? But I've told him I cannot accept it."

"Why not?"

"I – I don't want to be beholden to him! He will take us over, Su – tell us what we may or may not do with our lives. I want to be free of him. I love him, of course, but I want us to be equals."

"But you are not equals. He is wealthy and we are poor."

"We have money saved!"

"But there is little enough. And thou hast no work. And this child – his grandchild – will soon be born."

She was practical, like him. She did not see the loss to my pride.

"I have told him no. I rejected his help once, and said I'd make my own way. I will not turn to him now."

"Oh, Will!" Her voice rose, and I felt her impatience with me. "Thou'rt so stiff and proud – it is ungodly! He wants to help thee. Let him give thee money; it is how he shows his love for thee. Thou hurt him by rejecting it. Be gracious and accept."

She trembled as I stared at her, but her expression was resolute.

"I am right," she said. "I have never been more sure of it."

Her words found their mark. "Yes," I said at last. "Thou'rt right. I *did* hurt him. I will tell him I have changed my mind."

She came and embraced me. "Tell him too that next summer we will travel to Shropshire and show him his grandchild. It is what he wants, more than anything."

My father left next day. He would meet with other merchants in Oxford and be home within a week. Susanna and I went down together into the yard to wish him Godspeed. He looked at the two of us, smiled and shook his head.

"You are such children!" he said. "So young for all this. And you think you can create a new world."

Then he kissed us both, and said, "Come soon to Hemsbury. We will expect you."

Susanna

For the hand of Judith Kite,
at the Forge in Lower Street, Boston, Massachusetts.
The twentieth day of February, 1667.

Dearest Friend,

I write with great joy to tell thee of the birth of our
son, whom we have named Josiah. He was born two
weeks ago, here in Mile End, after a long and difficult
labour which left me grateful to God for my life and
that of my child. He is a healthy babe, strong and, I
think, already with a look of his father about him. It is
so strange and wonderful to be a mother. The night
after he was born I lay looking at him swaddled in his
cradle, and felt myself no longer one person, but

connected, through him, to the past and the future. Oh, I hope – I believe – the future will hold great things for Josiah!

I must tell thee, Judith, about his cradle. It was sent to me by Will's father, and is the Heywood family cradle in which Will's own mother rocked him. It is carved of dark oak, with a border of leaves and berries. I thought most tenderly of Henry Heywood for sending it; he calls me daughter now and, I believe, is reconciled to me.

In the summer we shall go to Shropshire and visit both our families. Will's father will pay. I long to see my own parents and Deb, and thou may be sure I will call on thy family too and give thee news of how they all look.

It has been a hard winter, uncommon cold, and with much snow. Hard especially for the poor people of London who have been made homeless and are without work. Will has had to take whatever employment he can. He wrote letters for people after the fire, and helped with claims and searches; and for a while he was one of those who dug and cleared rubble in the streets of London. Now he works some nights at a tavern but he has also begun helping Nat at his new premises in

Stepney, which is less than a mile from here.

Nat is one of the few who did not suffer from the fire, except in the loss of some possessions. He had already signed the lease of his workshop, and now he has gained the custom of many who lost their London printers. Amos Bligh lost all his plant and stock. He has gone back to his home town of Watford and seems unlikely to return. Nat has taken on one of Amos's printers as well as an apprentice. He intends next year to open a stationer's and wants Will to manage this. In time they hope to have a bookshop like Mary's. There is a need for a stationer's here, so we hope it will be profitable. Nat is happy. He is his own master, and doing God's work. He said to us once, "I've never wanted to go out and preach the Word, only to live it through honest trading." And he is a good and honest man.

Rachel comes to see me whenever she can. She is forced now to lodge with her mother in Houndsditch and often complains of it. I believe it will not be long before she marries Nat. I know he wishes it; he pursues her discreetly. I hope it will come to pass; then the four of us may work and bring up our children together.

I told thee soon after the fire that we had come

here to lodge in a small room at our Friends the Goodwins'. It is well enough, but I must share the kitchen with Margaret Goodwin and that is not easy. We both try to see the light in each other but sometimes we fail. At these times I tell myself that all the parishes outside the city walls are full of displaced people and that we have been luckier than some others. Rents are now high, and many have had to move out of London and seek work and housing elsewhere.

But now here is good news: Will and I are to move to a place of our own in Mile End Green — only two rooms, but one is a kitchen, and both rooms are on the ground floor. It backs onto orchards and fields, which will be healthy for the child. I long to move and begin to make a home for us again.

What times we have lived through, Judith! The persecution of our people here has eased, but none of us believe it will not begin again. There is a large and loving meeting here in Mile End Green, and Friends in Ratcliff and Stepney and all around. We will endure. We have come through persecution, plague and fire, and will live and work in the truth.

Write to me soon, dear friend, and tell me all thy

news. I think often of thee and Daniel and little
Benjamin. An ocean lies between us, but in our hearts
we can reach across it. And who knows but some day we
may meet again?

God keep thee, Judith, and hold thee in the light.

Thy friend,
Susanna Heywood

ABOUT THE AUTHOR

Ann Turnbull was brought up in Bexleyheath, London, but now lives in Shropshire. She has always loved reading and knew from the age of ten that she wanted to be a writer. Her numerous books for young readers include *Pigeon Summer*, *Deep Water*, *Room for a Stranger*, *No Friend of Mine* and *No Shame, No Fear*, which was shortlisted for both the Whitbread Children's Book Award and the Guardian Children's Fiction Prize in 2004.

Forged in the Fire, the sequel to *No Shame, No Fear*, continues the story of Will and Susanna. Ann says, "As soon as I finished writing *No Shame, No Fear* I knew I had to find out what happened to them – and when the book was published a flood of emails from readers showed that they felt the same. I had known all along that Will and Susanna would be caught up in the terrible events of 1665–66. It was challenging and exhilarating to try to recreate that time."

Find out more about Ann Turnbull and her books by visiting her website at www.annturnbull.com

ANN TURNBULL

NO SHAME, NO FEAR

A novel of love and persecution

It is 1662 and England is reeling from the after-effects of civil war, with its clashes of faith and culture.

Seventeen-year-old Will returns home after completing his studies to begin an apprenticeship arranged by his wealthy father.

Susanna, a young Quaker girl, leaves her family to become a servant in the same town.

Theirs is a story that speaks across the centuries, telling of love and the struggle to stay true to what is most important – in spite of parents, society and even the law.

But is the love between Will and Susanna strong enough to survive – no matter what?